THE SECRET SIBLING

Unexpected Magic #3

SAMANTHA JACOBEY

Lavish
Publishing LLC

Unexpected Magic #3

First Edition

All Rights Reserved

Published in the United States by Lavish Publishing, LLC, Midland, Texas

Paperback edition

ISBN: 978-1-64900-020-0

Cover Design by: Victor R. Sosa

Cover Images: Canstock

www.LavishPublishing.com

Contents

WALKING BETWEEN THE GUARDS, Morcant Korrigan ignored the noise of the prison surrounding him. His features sedate, he seemed in no hurry, ambling along with only his eyes darting to keep watch around his muscled form, his physique not bad for a man who's lived in excess of a century. He had been sentenced to life without possibility of parole a short two months prior, but the old witch had no intention of spending his next hundred years in that wretched place.

Arriving at the twenty-by-twenty room, four round tables with stools for seating occupied the barren space. The walls a dull gray, they matched his mood as he spied the lone figure occupying the visitation area. "All for me," he mused to himself with a grimace. The prison had held visitations to a bare minimum and those few were solo since the pandemic began, so he counted himself lucky to get this one.

"You got ten," his keeper informed him, indicating for him to join his guest.

Sauntering over the table, three large tomes held the center of the flat surface. Taking a seat, he growled, "They passed inspection?"

"Yes, they're letting you have them." His voice muffled by his mask, the man across from him appeared to have no opinion on the matter.

"Good." Morcant fingered a leather cover, noting that both had seen better days. "Did you have any issues getting them out of the shop?"

"No," his conscript replied. "We are in lockdown due to the pandemic. The store hasn't been open in months. No one saw me go in, and I doubt anyone will miss them."

"Excellent." Morcant sneered, laying his palm flat against the leather binding he had been fondling. "What about my brother?"

"He's playing house with the redhead, Sarah, and her friend, Karen."

Morcant's grin morphed into a scowl. "I heard about that. They have moved into my family dwelling."

"Yes," the visitor clipped. "Can you reach them from here?"

"Yes, but I have other plans at the moment. Once I am free of these bonds, I will recover the vessel that houses Brenna." He glanced around to see that they remained alone in room, save the two guards near the door. "Once my freedom has been won, then we may focus on completing her awakening."

"Of course, Magister." Tapping the table, the man fidgeted anxiously. "You have performed rituals here?" The visitor's voiced quavered doubtfully. "You'd need –"

"I have all that I need," Morcant interrupted, "besides

the spells. A guard has taken favor upon me, so I already possess all else that I require."

"You've been busy," the visitor surmised with a grin.

"Yes." Morcant also smiled deviously. "Soon, new witches will arrive. They are part of my plan and will serve me well. Make sure they acquire that which they seek."

The visitor nodded, seeing a guard indicating the time to leave. "Then I will return when I have news to report."

"Indeed," Morcant agreed. "But I warn you. You should not interfere with what I set in motion. Time is on my side. Days, weeks, and years of it. I intend to make the most of what I have, rest assured."

"How will I know if things are going all right, then?"

"Trust me." A guard arrived next to them, and Morcant hoisted his new books. "Thank you for the reading material, my friend."

"Reading material," the officer scoffed, eyeing the beat-up texts. "You have weird taste, my friend."

Morcant scowled at him, standing at full height to face him. "I am not your friend."

"You got that right," the guard continued to goad. "Let's go."

"I'll see you in a few weeks then," his visitor called after him as the coven leader reached the door.

"I wouldn't count on it," the guard shot back as they exited, the pair of uniforms laughing at what could only be an inside joke.

ONE

No Time
_____

WALKING HAND IN HAND, Rider Bradshaw tugged gently at his girlfriend's slender frame via the appendage. "That's the best," he mused, pointing at a balcony across the road.

"Uh…" She groaned. "I don't think so. I still like the one that had all the pink." Grinning behind her mask, Merideth Monroe considered Mardi Gras of the past. Last year, she had been new to New Orleans, so that first one had seemed magical. However, it had turned out to be a super-spreader event as the pandemic slammed NOLA hard on its heels, forcing the residents to shelter in place for months on end.

This year, with surges sweeping the nation and tourists still scarce, the old city had tried something new: Yardi Gras. She and Rider had even decorated their own balcony, and although she had little to compare it too, she thought the event had turned out a success. Frowning at his latest choice, she confirmed, "Definitely the pink one."

"You're too hard to please," he teased, pushing against her playfully with his shoulder. "How about we turn around and have some friend sex when we get home?"

"My, how suave." She giggled, enjoying his playful mood. They had always referred to their lovemaking in such a casual way, but lately she had begun to wonder if he would ever get past the 'friend' part. After over a year together, she had hoped to qualify as something more.

Stopping short, he spun her to face him, removing his mask at the same time. His lips ready to plant his kiss, he tugged her covering off her ear and panted, "What else is there to do?"

Lifting her chin, she closed the gap between them, the intimacy radiating around them. Any other time, their public display might have seemed ordinary, but in the midst of Covid, they stood out like a sore thumb. Passers-by cutting wide to the left or right, they lingered, the crowd grumbling at their interruption of their social spacing.

"Home then," she whispered when she broke the connection.

Pivoting, Rider reclaimed her hand and guided her expertly down the walk. Arriving at the bottom of their stairs a few minutes later, he released his grip and sent her up ahead of him. Enjoying the swish of her tight rear end as she climbed, he practically drooled.

Applying her key, Meri stumbled inside, the sound of a drop cloth crunching beneath her feet in the dimly lit room. "Watch my paint," she warned as he closed the door behind them.

"Sexy," he growled, catching her at the hallway and

lifting her to his chest. Carrying her the rest of the way, he dropped her across their bed, which stood in the last bedroom. Stripping off his hoodie, he could hear the thud of her shoes hitting the floor. "Lights?" he asked while tugging at his belt.

"No," she panted, also removing clothing as quickly as she could.

Sprawling across her, his briefs stretched tight across his throbbing member. "I love you, Meri," he breathed into her ear.

"Yeah, I love you, too," she agreed, stifling a sigh beneath her desire. Tugging at the elastic waistband, she groaned, "You're not ready."

"Oh baby, I'm ready," he pronounced, yanking at the covering to remove it. Plunging inside her, he pumped vigorously.

Lying beneath him, Meri grunted, going through the motions. Once, she had felt lost in loving him, but her mind had been trapped in too many other things lately to give herself to him completely.

From the front room, chimes began to play.

"Shit." Merideth pushed against his shoulders. "That's my phone," she huffed.

"Forget it. You can call them back," he pleaded into her hair.

"I can't. That's my father's ringtone." Kicking her feet, she fought to dislodge him. "Please, Boo. I need to get that."

Rolling off her, Rider ran his fingers through his hair as he glared at the dark ceiling above them. Her bare feet patting the hardwood floor as she traversed the hall, he listened, his pulsing organ impatiently waiting for her return.

"Hello? Are you there?" She panted heavily, pulling on the robe she had snatched from the hook on their door on her way by. "Yeah, I'm fine."

"You sound out of breath," Garrett Monroe accused over the line.

"I had to run to get to the phone," she replied calmly, fighting to slow her lungs. "What's going on?"

"Well, things were the same at the doctor this morning. There hasn't been any reduction in the size of the tumor," her father stated bluntly.

"Are they giving up?" Meri gasped. Sinking down to perch on the edge of a chair, she tugged the cloth around her more tightly.

"No. They are going to run the next course of treatments…but it doesn't look good. Your mother has very little time, sweetheart."

"Oh my God." Tears streaked her cheeks. Staring at the dimly lit hallway, she knew Rider was still on the bed, waiting for her. The feel of the wetness between her legs made her uncomfortable with her father talking in her ear.

The pause grew long, and Merideth caught a ragged breath from the other end of the call. "Please, Daddy," she whispered. "You have to be strong. Mother needs you right now."

"I know she does," he sniveled. "But I'm losing her all over again. Only this time, it's slow, and I'm watching her disappear one treatment at a time."

"I know it's hard," she soothed.

"Come home, pumpkin." His voice quavered and he waited for her reply.

"You know I can't do that," she replied gently.

"Yes, you can. Fuck the pandemic," her father shouted in her ear. "You get on a plane and you come home. That easy. Your mother has no time, love. If you want to see her again, you'll make it happen. You know she wants you to be here."

Meri knew exactly that. Ezamay Monroe had asked her to return to Virginia every time they had spoken since her cancer had been discovered almost six months earlier, but so far Meri had refused the invitation.

"I'll think about it," she replied crisply. Standing, she ended the call and dropped the device on the table and her robe onto the floor. Stomping down the hall, she found Rider lying sprawled across the bed where she had left him.

Flopping herself over him, she demanded, "Let's fuck."

"That's what we were doing," he shot back, flipping her over and tucking her beneath him. Back inside her, he thrust full force against her.

"Harder," she begged, lifting her feet towards the ceiling. Grinding her teeth, she urged, "Fuck that pussy."

"So nasty." He slapped against her, catching her legs behind the knees and forcing them down to fold her in half.

"Hurt me. That's it. Oh, dear God," she moaned.

His hands squeezing harder, he couldn't hold back the rush. "Ugh, not yet," he groaned. Too late, he convulsed. "I wasn't ready." His deposit squished as he slipped out of her. "You're lucky I couldn't hold it."

"Were you going to put me on my knees?" she

clipped, rolling onto her belly and grinding against the comforter.

"Are you still on about that?" he demanded. Grabbing her arm, he tried to roll her to face him, but she pulled away. On her feet, she stomped out the door.

"I'm first in the shower," she called, slamming the door.

Alone in their room, Rider sat back on his haunches, the mattress curved heavily between the weight of his knees. "Damn." When they first became lovers, it had never been like this. Everything changed when her mother became sick. Sweet tender love making. That was his Meri. Now it was like he hardly knew her.

Grabbing his underwear, he used them to clean himself, then pulled on his jeans raw. Thinking about her behavior, his gut ached. Only a few nights before, she had asked him to do things to her he had never done to anyone. Nasty things. Things he would never dream of doing to someone he cared so deeply for.

Stomping to the kitchen, he started a pot of coffee and watched it trickle into the carafe. "Please, just let us make it through this," he whispered aloud. The two of them had a great life coming, but first they had to get past her mother's illness. "I know that's why she's so torn up."

Down the hall, the water cut off. Not waiting for her to join him, Rider poured a generous cup and moved to wait at the closed portal. When she opened it, he stepped forward, preventing her exit. "What did your father say?" he demanded.

"Nothing."

"Don't give me that. I can tell something's wrong, Meri."

"Move," she huffed.

"Not until you level with me." Grasping her shoulder, he squeezed firmly, then massaged. Offering her the mug, he grinned. "Coffee?"

Glaring at him, she sighed loudly, shrugging to remove his hand. Taking the hot liquid, she slurped it, then explained in a hushed voice. "My father is having a hard time dealing with it."

"He's not the only one," Rider observed quietly. "What's the doctor say?"

"She isn't getting any better," she clipped.

"We should go," he informed her, his voice still low. "I know you don't want to, but Boo, we need to face this."

Her chin dimpled, then quivered. "I can't, Rider."

"Going doesn't mean you're giving up on her. It will show how much you care," he informed her gently. Drawing her into an embrace, he held her as her body jerked. When the tremors had subsided, he added more firmly, "I'm taking you home. I'll rent us a car if you don't want to fly."

"You would drive all the way to Virginia?" She sniffed, wiping at her pink-colored nose.

"Boo, I would drive around the world for you."

Her eyes flickering up at him, she could see the tenderness his blue orbs held. Knowing how much he loved her, and how much this meant to her parents, she had no excuse to delay any longer. "Ok, I'll pack a few things and you can arrange the flight. No sense in spending days driving."

"Do I get a shower before we go?" he teased, locating his phone.

Meri bit her bottom lip, wishing she hadn't rushed him. "I think we will have time for another round before we leave, so I wouldn't bother." Swaying her hips, she sauntered down the hall to take care of the chores before she changed her mind.

TWO

Secrets Past

"ARE you sure you're good with flying?" Rider asked as they entered the airport.

"Yes." Merideth hoisting her bag further up on her shoulder. "This will be quicker. The sooner we get there, the sooner we can come home."

Rider felt a twinge in his gut at her use of the word *home*. She had lived with him for over a year, but lately he wondered if she regretted that choice. "We can stay as long as you need to. The gallery is still closed, and I can draw anywhere."

Boarding the plane a short time later, Meri took the window and did her best not to sulk. Her hand wrapped in his across the armrest, she wished they had something to talk about to distract them, but lately there had only been bad news to discuss. Glancing around at the masked faces that surrounded them in first class, she realized it wasn't only happening to them. Lots of people were sick, and many had dying parents to worry about. In the pandemic, her suffering wasn't special, and that made it hurt all the more.

Landing a few hours later, Rider helped carry the bags to the rental counter, where they picked up a car. A dark gray sedan, the enormous trunk dwarfed their few belongings. "You could have brought half your closet," Rider teased, hoping to lift her spirits.

Appreciating his effort, Merideth managed a small smile. "I should have brought an empty suitcase and done some shopping instead."

"Now there's an idea. Maybe we can spend a few days in the city before we fly home. I could use a vacation after all these months as a shut in."

"You and me both." She rolled her eyes but giggled. Closing the distance between them, she presented herself for affection, which he showed her with strong arms and a lingering kiss. "Thank you," she murmured when he broke the connection.

"For what, Boo?"

"For your support. I've been mentally challenged, and you have been more than understanding." She inhaled deeply, ready to face the inevitable. "Shall I drive?"

"If you want," he replied, offering her the key.

Accepting it, she grinned at the fob. "It's a pushbutton start, isn't it."

"Yup. Kind of makes me miss the good old days." He rounded the passenger side and climbed in. Adjusting the seat, he took a reclined position as she slid behind the wheel and made her own accommodations. Comfortable, he watched her, wondering how well she would hold up if things with her mother were as bad as he feared they were.

Parking in front of her mother's house, Meri gripped the wheel, squeezing it with white knuckles. The closer they got, the slower she had driven, but eventually the distance had been covered. Glancing at the front windows, she caught movement at one of them, bringing a small smile to her lips. "They were waiting for us."

"Of course, they were," Rider agreed. Climbing out and stretching, he went around to the trunk and retrieved their bags.

Meri exited the sedan but hadn't reached the door before it swung wide, and both her parents emerged. Accepting hugs from each of them, she clung to her mother for a moment before letting her go. Stepping back, she inspected her frail frame.

"I know I'm a sight," Ezamay offered. "But I haven't given up!"

"That's good, Mother. Shall we go inside?"

"I'll help with the bags," Garrett offered as Rider slammed the trunk closed.

"That won't be necessary," the younger man instructed as he joined them. "We traveled light."

Merideth's father scowled at the small pair of suitcases. "I see," he hissed, surmising that she didn't plan to stay near as long as he had hoped.

Inside, the couple went up to her old room, which had been converted to a guest quarters almost as soon as she had left home. With little remaining to remind her of the past, she slouched onto the edge of the bed and grimaced at the decor.

"We should go down and join them. That's why we're here," Rider prodded.

"I know." She sighed. "I'm not sure how this is going to go, that's all. She cleared me out and dismissed me when I went to college. It feels weird being back here."

"It's only a visit. Maybe the last you will have with her, so make the best of it," he suggested.

Downstairs, the couple joined her parents in the den, and again Meri felt strange being there. Standing in the same room where her mother had presented her with their family diary a few years before, she shuddered.

"Are you cold?" Garrett asked, noticing her discomfort. "We can light the fireplace," he offered.

"That sounds great," Rider chimed in. "I love the smell of burning wood."

Happy for the distraction, Merideth agreed. Helping with the chore, the trio set the blaze while Mrs. Monroe curled beneath a blanket on the sofa.

Once the walls were doused in dancing light, the rest settled into chairs that completed the circle around the large hearth. Outside, the temperature dropped as the sun set, the blaze only a small amount of comfort.

"When is your next treatment?" Rider asked, breaking the awkward silence.

"I had one the day before yesterday and will go again the day after tomorrow," Ezamay supplied.

"The day after tomorrow," Meri repeated in a quiet whisper.

"They only do two a week," her father explained. His brow knitted, he waited to see what their only child would say next.

But Merideth didn't say any more. Her eyes glazed,

her expression hard to read, she sat stiffly in her chair until they were summoned to dinner.

Catching her arm as they followed her parents into the dining room, Rider hissed in her ear. "You need to relax. Your mother wants to see you."

"Of course, she does," Garrett barked, having overheard the suggestion.

"She does what?" Ezamay asked, placing her napkin in her lap as she settled into her chair.

"You want to see her," Rider clarified, his voice raised slightly. Taking in each Monroe in turn, he noted that his beloved wasn't the only one who seemed on edge. Recalling how they had met, he added, "Have you visited with any of your family?"

"No." Ezamay laughed at the question. "Have you seen any of yours?" She cut her eyes over at her daughter, her curiosity surfacing. "Or have you put any work into your part of the diary?"

"We are non-practicing," Merideth informed her mother crisply.

"Non-practicing?" Garrett paused in filling his plate to join the conversation. "What exactly does that mean?"

"It means they have chosen to ignore the craft," Ezamay informed her mate gently.

"Ah, then I believe that is a good thing." He resumed adding items to his china. "I find it gratifying that my daughter chooses to base her life on reality rather than mysticism."

Rider noted Ezamay's flushed cheeks. "Are you all right?"

"I'm fine." She coughed, then reached for her glass. Gulping a few large swallows, she returned the crystal to the flat surface before informing Garrett in a loud tone, "The craft is not so frivolous as you make it sound, dear."

"Is that so," her husband spat, pointing at her with his fork. "I suppose you could whip up a spell to remove your tumor, should I allow it. Is that it?"

Merideth gaped at them. Her mouth open in awe, her mind raced. "How long have you two been fighting about this?"

"We aren't fighting," her father snapped. "I have my opinion and she has hers. That does not imply that a quarrel has ensued."

Pressing her lips together, Meri felt certain the exact opposite to be true. "Do you think you could heal yourself?" She turned her attention to her mother, a glimmer of hope twisting her gut.

"I'm afraid not." Ezamay's clear blue eyes watered, and she swiped at her cheek. "I haven't practiced in years, and I'm afraid burying my talents has left me with little use for magic."

"But you made that one spell," Rider interrupted. "The binding." His comment fell flat across the table as he glanced at his lover. "The one that healed the rift between our families," he clarified.

"I had significant help with that."

"Can we please not rehash my wife's role as a witch?" Garrett demanded. "Her skills, if you care to call them that, are no match for a malignant cancer."

"But what if they are?" Meri breathed, taken with the idea. "Or maybe Rider and I could help."

"You'll do no such thing!" Garrett's fist met the table with a loud thud. "I asked you here to comfort her, not to…" His voice trailed away.

"But it could be worth a try," Rider seconded. "I mean, just because we helped with this doesn't mean we would be taking up that lifestyle afterwards."

Ezamay's lips thinned into a grin. "Bless you, Rider Bradshaw. You always were a generous boy." Her gaze flittering to Meri, she inhaled deeply. "I'm afraid this isn't the kind of thing we can fight with spells. Even if my daughter is willing to break her vow to do so." She glared at Garrett, anger swirling in their depths.

Merideth swallowed heavily. "Thank you, Mother. I'm glad you understand."

"Oh, I understand. And while there isn't much we can do about my illness, I do actually have a task for you, if you accept it," Ezamay proposed, releasing her mate from her fowl gaze.

Cutting her eyes over, Meri glared at the older woman. "What sort of task? I mean, the last one you sent me on nearly killed me."

Nodding, Ezamay shrugged. "What's an old woman to do?"

Rider spat a small laugh at the comment. "You aren't that old," he corrected.

"As you say. Nonetheless, I'm afraid I don't have time to debate my years," she acquiesced.

"Please don't do this," Garrett interrupted. Glaring at his wife, he waited. "You promised."

"I never promised," Ezamay denied, sliding back in her seat and folding her arms over her chest. "Besides, I'm the one who is dying. I have a right to my final wishes."

Meri's eyes flooded with tears. "Oh, Mother. Please, ask and if I can, I will certainly try."

"You aren't going to like this," Garrett warned. Getting to his feet, he applied his cloth napkin to his lips and dropped it over his half-finished plate.

"Where are you going?" Meri demanded, pushing back her chair as if to follow.

"Let him be," Ezamay suggested as he exited the room. "This has hurt him. My illness and the favor I would ask of you."

"I know." Meri sighed, lifting her fork to toy at her meal. "Our family has never been strong on emotion. We may feel it, but we certainly never show it."

"I do regret that." Her mother nodded. "It has led to many secrets and hard feelings."

"Pfft, secrets," Rider parroted between bites. "My dad is full of them."

"Yes, this is one of his as well," Ezamay informed him crisply, bringing his chewing to a halt. She waited until his eyes met hers, then explained, "Your father and I have a complicated history."

"Do tell." He swallowed, reaching for his glass. "I thought you spilled it all after our little adventure last time."

"Hardly." Ezamay laughed, then coughed. Downing a few more swigs of water, she quieted the spasm. "Teddy and I had a child together. A secret child."

"What?" Merideth gasped. "When the hell was this?"

"After Rider's mother...erm...died. Before I married your father. I told you about our romance."

"Romance yes, but a child?" On her feet, Merideth stomped over to the door, then pivoted to face the pair at the table. "Did you know about this?"

"Me?" Rider squeaked, opening an empty palm.

"How would I know about this? My father is a conniving old bastard. He doesn't tell me anything…unless it's convenient." Turning to Ezamay, he added, "Why don't you just ask your favor and quit messing with her head?"

"I need you to find my first daughter," Ezamay stated flatly. "I wish to speak with her before I die."

THREE

Winding Paths

ALONE IN GARRETT'S STUDY, Rider fumed. Pacing back and forth, he hoped to calm his frayed nerves, but quickly realized delaying the call only made them worse. Pulling his cell out of his pocket, he muttered to himself as he scrolled the short list of numbers. Locating the one belonging to Thaddeus Bradshaw, he hit the send and placed the device to his ear to listen.

"Rider, my boy! How are things down in NOLA?"

"How should I know?" Rider bit tartly. "I'm in Virginia, visiting with Ezamay."

"Oh," Thad replied, his voice dropping a few levels. "How's the old girl doing?"

Rider winced. "She isn't old. And she isn't likely to ever be." Inhaling sharply, he fought for control. "That's not why I called, Dad."

"You called about your sister," his father stated at near a whisper.

"Yes. I'm not even going to ask how you know that. Honestly, I'm surprised you wouldn't deny it." Running his fingers through his hair, Rider exhaled a long blow. Calmer, he continued, "Meri's mother wants to see her eldest daughter before she dies."

"I'm sure she does. It was hard as hell on her the day we decided to give Joseline away." Teddy's voice cracked when he said his daughter's name.

"Why do you always have to lie, Dad?" Rider blinked back tears. "Why can't you just tell me the truth?"

"There are things you aren't meant to know," his father soothed. "I know that's hard to understand."

"Like mom?"

"What about your mom?"

"Ezamay. She said mom died. But the way she said it was more like she was trying to remember what I'd been told."

"Ah." Thaddeus huffed into the phone. "It's complicated, son."

"With you, it always is. Look. You can explain my mother later. Right now, I need to know where to find this Joseline." Rider tapped his foot anxiously, waiting for the reply.

"That's complicated, too," Thad finally replied. "You better come here, and I'll see what I can find to help you."

"Great. No promises, Dad," Rider snapped before ending the call. Leaving the study, he found Meri and her mother back in the den, but Garrett was nowhere to be seen. "Is your dad still upset?"

"My father has gone out for the afternoon," Meri informed him, then sniffed. Doing her best to hide her tears, she added, "Did yours have any advice?"

"He had a name. Joseline. Other than that, he wants us to go there," he informed the women flatly."

"Joseline," Ezamay whispered. "How beautiful."

"You didn't know her name?"

"No. We realized before she was born that we couldn't keep her. It was better that we didn't name her." Her lip trembled and Ezamay bit it, holding it in place.

"Then how does he know her name?" Rider asked in frustration.

"Rider. I'm afraid there are things about your father you may not be aware of," the older woman pacified.

"Spare me," he grunted. "Not being aware? Forgetting to mention a parking ticket. That's not being aware. My father –"

"Is a good man," she cut him off. "Please don't speak ill of him in my presence."

Rider clamped his mouth shut, swallowing his harsh words. "Yes, ma'am. I'm sorry. I know you must still love him very much. It's just that I had a sister. My whole life, he never told me. I had a sister." He stopped there, his face losing its color.

"Boo? What's the matter?" Merideth closed the distance between them, worry etched on her delicate features.

"I have a sister, who is also may girlfriend's sister," he explained. "I have to admit, I'm a little disturbed by that right now."

"What, like we're committing incest?" Meri gasped. Glancing at her mother, she scowled. "We're not, are we?"

"No, the two of you are not blood related to each other. But he's right, you share a sibling."

"A secret sibling," Rider added hoarsely.

"I think I need a drink." Merideth left him and opened the bar on the far wall, across from the fireplace.

"I'll take one as well. Bourbon if you got it," he huffed.

Pouring each of them a double, Merideth gulped hers, then topped up her glass.

Swirling his, Rider admired, "I love a woman who can hold her liquor."

"Thanks." She grinned at him, her disgust at their possible relations waning. "When do we go to see your father?"

"Tomorrow, I guess. Unless you want to spend a few days here before we tackle the next challenge." He raised his glass to Ezamay as a toast. "We did come here for a visit, after all."

"Nonsense," Ezamay replied. "Please. Go and see if Teddy can help you bring my Joseline back to me."

Pulling up in front of his father's house, Rider placed the gear in park but didn't move. Not looking at Meri, he fidgeted with his jacket and then the steering wheel.

"Are we not getting out?" she demanded.

"Just…give me a minute." He continued to caress the leather covering. "I like this car. We should get us one when we get home."

"What about your bike?"

"My bike is nice, but it's not really a family vehicle." He didn't look at her, continuing to squirm.

"A family!" She gasped. "Rider what are you saying, and why are you saying it?"

"Because I'm scared," he spat, cocking his head to look at her. "We're going in that house and that crazy old man…" His voice trailed away as he pointed at the small porch. "He's going to say things we have no choice but to believe. I call him my Dad, but over the last couple of years I've come to realize he's not my family. You're my family." He held her gaze, waiting for her reply.

"Rider, I don't know what to say," she breathed. She had longed for this, but now?

"Then don't say anything, Boo." His fingers found her face, and he gently trailed the edge of her jaw. "But know that I love you, no matter what happens or what we find out about this secret sister of ours."

"I know. I love you, too. We'll talk about this when we've finished my mother's task, ok?" She smiled, genuinely believing that they would.

"Yeah." He grinned back, tweaking her chin before exiting via his door. She waited dutifully and he opened hers, offering his hand to help her onto the curb.

"Such a gentleman." She looked up at him, waiting for his kiss, which he gently planted on her lips. "Your father is watching us."

"I know. Play it up."

"Shall we fuck on the hood?" She grinned deviously.

"Not that far." He chuckled, his face flushed at the thought. Taking her hand, he led her up the short walk and mounted the steps. At the screen, Thaddeus stood on the other side. "Hi, Dad."

"Hello, Son." Thad cut his eyes over at Meri, narrowing them slightly. "How's your mother?"

"She's strong, Thad. She's holding up."

He pushed the door open and allowed them to enter. Shuffling towards the kitchen, he mumbled, "Didn't take you long to get here."

"Ezamay is anxious to meet Joseline. We left first thing this morning," Rider informed him gruffly. "So where can we find her?"

"Well, I'm afraid that something's come up. After we spoke yesterday, I got to thinking about all those years ago," Thaddeus began.

"Don't bullshit me, Dad," Rider shouted. "Just tell me where she is and we'll be on our way."

"Honey," Meri soothed, massaging his arm. "I'm sure he's going to tell us what he knows."

"I'm not," Rider bit angrily.

"Well, you're right there," Thad agreed with a grin, nodding at his son. "I've changed my mind. She was placed in a good home with a good family. Trusted to an old friend of mine. I think it's better if she stays where she is and leave it at that. You can go have a holiday, maybe a week, then go tell Ezamay you couldn't find her."

"I'm not going to do that!" Merideth gasped. "I've always been honest with my mother. I'm not going to lie to her on her deathbed!"

"Honest." Thad sneered. "No one is honest. We all tell as much lie as we can get away with." He opened a beer, then held it out. "Anyone?"

"No, thank you. Look. What do you want? I'm sure there is a reason you aren't helping after you said that you would," Rider pleaded.

"There is and you don't need to know it," Thad clipped, chugging half the bottle.

"I think he's drunk," Meri observed quietly to her mate.

"Yeah. I'm inclined to agree." His eyes shifting around, he took in the small house. The kitchen and living area made up the front half, but the space was cramped with furniture and boxes, probably pulled from storage. His eyes making it to the couch, he noticed a carton of pictures that had been spilled onto the pliable surface.

Catching his gaze, Thaddeus headed him off. "Leave that be. It's none of your concern." Making it to the sofa ahead of him, Rider managed to see a few of the images before Thad snatched them away. "Those are mine, I said."

Rider studied him with doleful eyes, watching him scoop them into the box and close the lid. "How do you know her name?" he asked gently.

Thad held tightly to his container of treasures. "I shouldn't have told you that."

"Ezamay says you didn't name her," Rider insisted.

"We didn't," his father snapped. Box under his arm, he went in search of another beer.

"But you know her. How?" Rider glared at him, considering if the alcohol would make it easier or harder to get what they needed.

"I see things. I watch." Thad took a few swigs out of his fresh supply. "I'm a witch, you know? Not like the two of you. Hiding your talents."

Meri gasped, but Rider signaled her to remain silent.

Nodding her willingness to obey, she moved to the round wooden table and pulled out a chair.

"I can see you're upset, Dad. Tell me about it." Rider indicated the remaining seats. "Sit with us and let's have a talk."

"It's too late to talk. What's done is done. Digging up the past isn't going to help anyone."

"It will help my mother," Merideth interjected, unable to hold her tongue. "Please, Mr. Bradshaw. She's very sick. Her time is short. She has only asked for one small thing. It's not too much to ask; really, it isn't."

"You say that now, but will you when it's all said and done?" Thad raised the bottle and finished off the beverage. Throwing it into the trash with a loud bang, he shuffled over to the chair. Reaching into his pocket, he produced a glass ball, too large to be a marble. "You're a seer, Merideth Monroe. This I pass to you."

Opening her hand, Meri accepted the object, noting the weight in her palm. "What does it do?"

"Meri, I thought we agreed," Rider gently reminded her.

"I'm not using the craft," she assured. Smiling up at Thad, she prodded, "What does it do?"

"There are those who can look inside. Who sense what is around them. I have used this for many decades that I may watch what cannot be seen," he provided cryptically.

"It's a crystal ball," she gasped, noting a swirl forming inside it. To her surprise, a tall figure came into focus just before Rider snatched it away.

"We're non-practicing, remember?" He leaned over her, the warning puffing warm air against her forehead.

"I remember." Her words slurred and she shook her head to snap out of it. Deciding to keep the woman in the glass to herself, she turned to Rider's father. "Thank you. If there is anything else you would like to tell us, we would appreciate it. But if you won't, we will find another way."

"Another way," he echoed, distraught. "Why can't you leave it alone?"

"Because my mother has tasked me with this. I have disappointed her so much in my life, I can't let her down now. I need to make things right between us before she's gone," Meri explained firmly.

"And you think your sister will help." Teddy laughed. "She won't. But I guess you need to discover that for yourself." He turned his back on them, opening the fridge and rummaging inside. "M & J's. That's where you should start. Morcant and Judoc Korrigan were friends of ours back in the day. They took the baby the night she was born." Pulling out a cold steak, he placed it in the microwave. He tapped the one, and the device hummed to life. "They were to find a home for her. A family to call her own."

Rider swallowed; his gut twisted. "Where?"

"Boston. Their shop is a gathering place. They head a coven. I can't promise they will help you, but it's a start." He winked at Merideth. "Or, you could simply let your girl here have the glass and look for herself."

"We don't need magic," Rider insisted. "M & J's. Morcant and Judoc. How original. It should be easy to find them." Turning on his heel, he exited via the screen door, fully expecting Merideth to follow.

FOUR

Life on Hold

"OH MY GOD, can you believe all this dust?" Sarah called to her friends as she tended to yet another shelf of books.

"We haven't been here in months, what did you expect?" Blake teased. Behind the register, he busied himself inventorying their supplies. "We'll need more register tape."

"Got it," Karen replied, adding it to her list. Chewing the cap on her pen, she appeared pensive.

"What are you thinking about now?" Sarah demanded. "And why aren't you helping me clean?"

"Dust makes me sneeze," Karen replied tartly. "And I'm busy thinking about names."

"Names for what?" Blake asked, pausing his count of bags and boxes to swipe his sweaty brow.

"The shop, silly. I'm sure you won't be calling it M & J's now that the M is gone," she shot back.

"Oh, yeah. About that." He beamed, motioning for

Sarah to drop her rag and join them. She moved to do so under the guise of needing a drink, grinning from ear to ear.

"What about it?" Karen urged. "Have you already come up with one?"

"Maybe." Sarah giggled, unable to control her joy. "Blake wants to make us his partners."

Karen's face instantly fell. "Shit."

"Shit what?" Sarah exclaimed, clapping her hands. "I thought you would be happy!"

"I am happy." Karen forced a smile. "For you. That's great news."

"What about you?" Sarah's features crumbled, aware that her best friend's reaction was not what she had hoped for. "You don't look pleased."

"I'm in shock, that's all." Karen swiped a cloth off the counter. "I'll start on the far wall."

"Not until you tell me what is going on," Sarah demanded, moving to block her path.

"I'm going home, Sarah." Her words filled the room and echoed loudly in her own ears. "We graduate in a few weeks, and after that, I'm going back to Atlanta."

Sarah blinked at her, unable to think. "After all we've been through?" she finally managed. "We almost died."

"Yeah. I know." Karen toyed with the rag. "But we didn't. Our lives have moved on, or at least yours has." She indicated Blake, who had returned to his counting on the other side of the sales desk. "The pandemic put everyone's life on hold, and I'm ready to get back to mine." Pushing past her, she limped heavily as she made her way across the open space and around Morcant's table.

Careful not to touch their previous magister's furniture, she reached the back wall and began removing the over-sized tomes.

"I can't believe she's leaving," Sarah breathed.

Standing to join her, Blake leaned against the flat surface between them. "She's lonely. This shutdown has been hard on us, but we had each other. She's had no one for months now."

"She had us, too," Sarah defended, tears dripping onto her cheeks.

"It's not the same." Grasping her hand, he squeezed. "Give her some time. She might come back."

"I can't even go to visit her." Sarah sniffed. "I can't go visit my own parents," she stated more forcefully.

"Why not?"

"Why not?" she shouted, indicating her bright red locks. "I don't look like me, remember? I'm a short fat girl with dark hair, or at least I used to be."

"You could explain it," Karen soothed, returning to the conversation.

"Yeah. Hey Mom, I'm a witch. I was possessed last year and totally have a new look, but I'm still me. I promise. Yeah, that'll go over well." Her face flushed, she couldn't decide whether to be angry or stick to the crying.

"It'll be tough," Blake agreed. "Give it some time, and we'll think of a good way to break it to them. For now, let's get this done so we can get out of here," he suggested, returning to his work.

Hours later, the trio left the shop and arrived at Blake's family dwelling. A massive old house, it had been built nearly two centuries before. Updated a few times over the years, it held all the modern conveniences, but Karen had never felt at home there.

Going straight up to her room, she busied herself with a shower and pajamas, then sat on her bed and contemplated reading or getting some sleep. After about half an hour, she got to her feet and took her cane as she made her way downstairs. Arriving at the kitchen, she found Blake and her best friend speaking in low tones.

Helping herself to a mug of the coffee they had brewed, she took the seat between them. "I'm sorry I didn't tell you guys what I was planning."

"It's ok," Blake offered right away. His long arm swinging over her head, he patted her on the back, then gave her a firm rub. "I didn't expect you to stay here forever." He cut his girlfriend a glare, waiting for her to agree.

Sarah didn't budge.

"I'll come back for a visit. I promise," Karen reassured, heaping on the sweet. "Sarah, I need you to understand."

"I get it!" Sarah held up her hand in a stopping motion. "We spent our senior year on Zoom, along with the rest of our campus. But there are men here, you know?"

Her jaw dropped as Karen studied her. "You think I'm going home in search of a boyfriend?" Shaking her head, the words to explain how deeply the notion hurt escaped her. "I'm sorry, Sarah. I can't say it enough. I don't belong here anymore. I need to go and discover who I am."

Sarah shrugged. "Fine." On her feet, she left the room and stomped up the stairs.

"She took that well," Karen lamented, then sipped loudly from her cup.

"Give her time. She'll be fine. And we'll figure out a way to get her back in with her parents. You do you, ok?" Blake smiled at his former conscript.

"How will you guys rebuild the coven without me?"

"We'll manage," he assured. "There will always be a place for you though, if you change your mind."

"Thanks." She finished off the hot liquid and stood, using her cane to make her way up to bed.

Waiting a few minutes, Blake contemplated what Karen's departure would mean. He had said they would be fine. What else could he say? In reality, her departure would have to be dealt with, if not then, at some point down the line.

When he had waited long enough, he placed their mugs in the sink and made his way upstairs, noting the dark space under Karen's door signaling that she had already crashed. "Poor kid. Today really wore her out," he mumbled to himself. Grinning deviously, he knew he and Sarah wouldn't go to sleep for hours.

Pushing their bedroom door open in a rush, he stepped inside, resisting the urge to slam it for the other girl's sake. "You're dirty," he observed, as Sarah had flopped across their bed without bothering to undress.

"So are you," she replied, her voice muffled by the mattress.

"Sure am," he agreed, loosening his belt. "You want to talk about Karen?"

"Nope."

"Good." He yanked the belt free. Folding it in half, he smacked her across the ass with a loud pop.

Rolling onto her side, her eyes wide, she glared at him. "Did I ask you for that?"

"No, but you needed it. Get undressed." His Adam's apple bobbed as he swallowed, his gaze boring into her.

"You first," she croaked, her butt cheeks still burning.

Tugging his shirt over his head, Blake bared his chest, then ran his fingers across the hairs that decorated it. Sarah groaned, flopping onto her back and tugging at the button of her jeans. Not waiting for their removal, Blake straddled her, his lips scorching as he kissed her. Gripping a hand full of flame-red hair, he pulled firmly.

"Karen's already out, so we should keep it down."

Sarah grunted, her anger still stirring within her. "Either take my clothes off or move so I can."

Slithering down her body, Blake stood at her feet. Grasping each foot in turn, he removed her shoes, then worked his way up. Her pants gone, he pushed his hands up her shirt to briefly tease her breasts. Standing, he tugged off his own jeans while she slipped out of what remained of her clothing, revealing the two red welts he had left on her backside.

"Oh, Baby, those must smart," he observed, his hand gliding lightly over them. "Want some more?"

"No, thank you. I'll settle for flesh."

"You got it." He smacked one of the streaks with a bare palm, instantly leaving a print over the top of the previous wound.

"Hey!" She squealed, on her face as she tried to wriggle away from him.

Undeterred, he pulled on her hips to get her knees under her, pushing himself inside. "Hey, what?" Using hard thrusts, he forced himself deeper.

Sarah ended her struggle and pushed back against him instead. "Ugh. I thought you were going in the other way."

"I am. We're just getting started," he assured her. Sucking his thumb to wet it, he pushed it into her puckered orifice. "We need the lube, though." He pumped against her, his digit pushing to stretch her.

Gripping the covers beneath her, Sarah groaned. "I used to be such a nice girl."

"You are a nice girl. Nice to fuck. Where's the lube?"

"It's on your side, I think." Adjusting her stance when he left her to go find it, her mind flittered to the night a stranger had been with her in much the same way. "When Brenna controlled me," she mumbled.

"What?" Blake asked, pushing objects around in the shallow drawer of his nightstand.

"Nothing," she muttered. "What's taking so long?"

"I can't find it."

"Well, let's go."

"Without? No way."

"Hey, my puss is plenty wet." She slithered her fingers between her legs to test it. "Just do that tonight."

"You want to have a baby?"

"Not particularly." She sighed. "Why can't we just use a condom."

"Because that's not the deal." He pulled the tube out and grinned. "Bingo."

Back inside her, he dripped the clear liquid onto her ring of pleasure. "You can suck me if you want." His fingers kneaded the flesh, two inside as he worked her, evaluating as he prepared her. "Almost there."

Moving in rhythm with him, she groaned. "Brenna made me nasty."

"Yes, she did, but you love it," he growled. Shifting himself, he massaged his way in. Applying more of the thick, cool liquid, he took more of her with every stroke. "Tell me when," he offered.

"I'm ok." Her eyes closed, she breathed deeply, letting the air out smoothly to slow her breathing. "Oh. OH." Her moans grew louder.

"I said say when," he insisted. His hands holding her hips on either side, he spread her more and watched as he moved in and out of her, almost fully penetrating. As much as he wanted to have a child with her, he loved fucking her ass. "How long?"

"Ugh, now!" Pushing her face hard into the mattress, her noises turned to high-pitched squeals.

"That's it, baby." He pumped against her, releasing inside her. "My nasty girl."

"Ohhh," she moaned, flexing her tingling fingers.

Climbing into the shower together a few minutes later, Blake used the soap, applying a thick lather to her body. "You feel good, Baby?"

"Oh yeah." Her smile genuine, she giggled. "Maybe tomorrow we can try for that baby you're always on about."

"You said that yesterday," he pointed out, rinsing his hands. He wasn't bitter. Hell no, fucking her was good either way. But he had begun to wonder if she ever would be ready.

"I'm still young," she pointed out as she cut off the spray. Reaching for a fluffy towel, she sighed. "I guess if

I were a hundred years old, I might feel the pressure, but right now I'm content to wait."

"I know. And I'm not pressuring you."

"Then don't," she clipped, cutting him off as she pulled her sleepshirt over her head and flopped into their bed.

FIVE

Guilty

MERIDETH SAT NEXT to Rider in near silence as they made the drive to Boston. "Thank you for not asking for another flight."

"No worries, Boo. It wouldn't save us much time anyway, and I know how badly you hate it."

"Mhmm," she agreed. Watching the terrain out the window, she sighed. Her first time in Rhode Island, she might have felt excited, but too many things pressed for her attention. Not to mention the small crystal that Rider hid in one of his pockets.

Biting her lip, she thought about the glass resting in her hand. It had felt heavy, the density of it greater than it appeared, as if it were lead rather than glass. More than she had expected, it called to her and she longed to hold it again. To explore the places it could take her.

But she and Rider had agreed they would remain non-practicing after the fiasco two years ago. Her mother's plan had worked out, and she had succeeded in not only healing the rift between their families but she had also helped her mother return from the dead. No small feat for a new witch.

"Why are you so scared of magic?" Meri asked aloud.

"What?" Rider stammered, thrown off by the randomness of her question. "What makes you think I'm scared of magic?"

Turning to gaze at his profile, she smiled. "Why else would you want to be sure I never partake in it? Was I so terrible with my wielding?"

"You weren't," he countered, inhaling sharply. Releasing the breath slowly, he searched for the right words. "I've been around casters my whole life. I know the pitfalls that await us if we go down that path. Sleezy dives. Unsavory characters. It gets brutal."

"Sounds like a normal day in America," she teased.

"Oh, you have no idea. There is a dark side to witch society I hope you never see."

Her mood sobered, her thoughts turned to the clash between their families. "Your wounds run deep. Maybe we will find a way to heal those while we are out on this little adventure."

"I'm terrified that's what your mother has in mind," he suggested calmly.

"Are you saying my mother is faking her illness?" She sat up straighter in her seat, her voice catching an edge. "Don't be coy. What are you accusing her of?"

"I'm not accusing her of anything, and I don't know that she is necessarily meddling, at least this time. But her track record isn't great, Boo." He glanced at her, visually checking her temperature before he added, "I wouldn't put it past her for this to be some kind of elaborate scheme."

"I bet, and don't Boo me when you're talking trash about my mother," she huffed. "If you had a long-lost daughter, I'm sure you would want to at least see, or maybe even just talk to her before you sailed off to the great beyond."

He laughed boldly. "I love the way you put things, and speaking of daughters, have you thought about my suggestion? What do you think about making this thing permanent?"

"What thing?" she snapped.

"Us. Of having a family together." He shrugged, playing it cool.

"I thought we had tabled that discussion until we were past all this," she reminded him, anger still putting an edge on her words.

"Well, how hard can it be? Dad gave us the guys who hid Joseline. They will know where she is, and I'm sure she will at least speak to Ezamay, if we can't outright take her to visit."

"And when has anything we have ever done been that easy?" She chortled at his naivety.

"I'm being optimistic. As I am with us. I think we make a great couple, and I'd like to hope we can make it more...sanctified." He shot her a quick grin, hoping to draw her in, or at least ease her down.

"Sanctified, as in matrimonial. Is this what you call a proposal?" She sounded less impressed by the minute.

"No, I'm not calling this a proposal. We're talking. I'm asking your opinion. What would you think about us…you know…getting married?" His patience growing thin, he bit the words off one at a time.

"I'm not sure what I think," she spat, crossing her arms and turning back to her window. They covered several miles before she had calmed enough to add, "I don't want to marry unless we are sure where we stand."

"You're not sure about us?" He sounded lost, as if even the thought of losing her pained him.

"I'm not sure our lives are going in the same direction. We were thrown together with the pandemic so soon after we started, and we haven't really lived a normal life together. Not yet." Her voice tender, she turned enough to face him and reached for his arm. "I'm not saying it's a bad idea, Boo."

"I have terrible timing," he muttered, shaking his head.

Smiling, she squeezed his appendage. "I think we will talk more about this. I know we will. You don't have to give up. You simply have to wait."

"I'll wait," he agreed quietly, hoping he really could.

"So, can you answer my question now?" Her voice took on a musical tone, as if she toyed with him.

"What question, Boo?"

"Why are you afraid for us to use magic?"

His features crumpled. "What does it matter? You got along your entire life without it, why is it so important that you use it now?"

Her heart thumped loudly in her ears. Did she tell him the truth, or should she let it go? She had kept her secret as long as she had known him. The changes had come on fast, after all, and her intuitions, as she like to call them, had only gotten stronger as time passed.

Maybe they had always been there, but without a name. Without definition that gave them clarity. Guilt twisted her gut at the thought of hiding what stirred within her from him.

"Well?" He glanced at her, emphasizing the word.

"This is it, isn't it. Either I trust you, or I don't," she whispered.

"What's that supposed to mean?"

"Something is happening to me, Boo," she confessed hoarsely. "I can't define it and I can't stop it."

"And you think it has something to do with magic." He rolled his eyes, his attitude not what she had hoped for.

"I don't know what's causing it. Maybe I'm just imagining it," she suggested. Turning back to the passing trees, she regretted reveling her secret. "Forget I mentioned it."

A tired hush fell over the couple, leaving a small chasm between them each found hard to overcome. It wasn't until they arrived at the edge of Boston that Rider hit upon a safe topic to broach.

"Care to navigate? Google M & J's for me and get the best route," he suggested.

"I can do that," she agreed readily. Using her cell, she located the store, then hit the blue button to begin the quest.

"Thanks, Boo," he said gently. "You're the best."

She flushed at his tenderness, aware that it would break her heart to leave him. She hoped he wouldn't pressure her to the point she had to. She wanted them to be more but it needed to be on her terms, and in her time.

Pulling up in front of the store a short time later, she

scowled. "Well, this can't be right. It says Spellbound Book Emporium. Not M & J's."

Rider stared at the sign atop a tall pole on the corner, then turned to view the storefront over his shoulder. "Let's get out."

"Why? This obviously isn't it." Irritation filled her voice. "I must have done something wrong," she lamented, handing him the device. "And even if it was it, the guys we need are probably no longer here."

Examining her entry, then rechecking the signs, he shrugged. "Maybe they changed their name, but it's still them. We won't know until we go inside." Handing her the cell, he turned up his collar to keep out the cool wind that cut across the nearly empty parking lot.

Clinging to her purse as she ran, her shorter legs pumped to catch him. He paused under the large sign on the eave to examine it from below. "It looks fresh. I'm betting they changed the name." When she arrived next to him, he pulled the glass entrance open so she could enter.

As soon as Meri crossed the threshold, a chill cascaded over her, the bell on the door etching fear into her gut. "I'm not sure about this, Boo," she repeated, her nails digging into her palms.

"About what." He grimaced, taking in the expanse of the shop. "It looks nice."

To their right, an old cash register adorned an ornate sales counter, dating the shop, but the rest had obviously been remodeled. Books lined rows of shelves, both straight ahead and to the left, but the left-hand wall held a huge display of crystals and amulets. "I like it. Looks comfy." He pointed to a ring of upholstered chairs that surrounded a large round coffee table.

"I thought you said magic shops were sleezy dives," she reminded him under her breath as a man about their age approached.

"Well, hopefully not this one," Blake rebuked. "Welcome to Spellbound."

SIX

Transformed

"THIS MAKES EIGHT CUSTOMERS TODAY," Sarah squealed as Blake made his way over to greet their new guests. "We'll be rebuilding the coven in no time!"

"If they aren't here to simply shop," Karen pointed out, a bit less enthusiastic. "She looks pretty tense."

At the door, Merideth stepped aside to give the guys room for their manshake, only half listening as they introduced themselves. Her eyes darting about her, her gut continued to twinge, and her intuition had leapt off the chart.

"I'm Rider Bradshaw." Their hands pumped vigorously.

"Blake Korrigan." He eyed the woman as he spoke. "You frequenting magic shops? I'm afraid we're still a bit dusty from the shutdown. This is only our second day with the doors open."

"Actually, no." Rider dropped the hand, queuing on the name. "We're here to see Morcant and Judoc. I assume you're a relative of theirs."

His lips puckered, Blake studied him, his eyes swiftly sweeping his tall frame from head to toe. "I'm afraid you've come to the wrong place. We're taking over the shop. Sorry." He indicated the two girls who whispered as they worked on a selection of books near the back of the store.

"Right, but you said your name is Korrigan. That's who we're looking for –"

"Morcant and Judoc Korrigan." Meri cut him off, her unease growing despite the bright décor. "Thaddeus Bradshaw sent us. He said they could help us."

Blake pursed his lips. "You related?" he mused aloud, raising his brows at Rider.

"Yes, he's my father. Look, I'm not trying to be pushy, ok? Can you just direct us to M & J? That's who we need to speak to." Irritation dripped from his lips.

"Welp, I'm afraid I can't help you there. Feel free to have a look around." Blake shoved his hands in his pockets, dismissing them. "Otherwise, have a nice day." Returning to his inventory list, he left them to their browsing.

"I don't like it here," Meri whispered loudly. "I told you this isn't the right place. We should go."

"Don't be hasty," Rider cautioned, wafting his hand around them. "He said we could have a look around. We've come a long way and this is the only clue we have."

"Clue." Blake sneered over his printout. "Sounds like you're off on one of those mystery adventure games."

"It's a game all right." Rider eased his way down one of the rows, inspecting the spines of some of the books. "Only we're the pieces."

Adjusting the strap to her purse anxiously, Meri moved towards the far side of the store, pausing when she reached the circle of chairs. Her leg brushed the hard wood of the table and the contact jolted her, as if lightning had passed between them, leaving her with a tingle. She jumped away by instinct, emitting a small yelp.

"You ok, Boo?" Rider called, his eyes still on the shelves.

"I'm fine. But this table is creepy."

"Creepy?" Blake laughed. "It's a table."

"No," she clipped. "It's dark. Evil." Her hand trembling, she leaned over, pressing the palm flat against it. "This is Morcant's table. I'm sure of it. I bet it was left here when they closed the shop." Looking over at Blake, she asked innocently, "Where did M & J go? Did they retire?"

Leaving the books, Rider scowled at her. "We're non-practicing, remember?"

Dropping her cleaning supplies, Sarah sauntered over to them, intrigued by her boyfriend's sidestep of the couple. "What does that mean, non-practicing?"

"It means, they are witches who are pretending not to be," Blake informed her with a sly grin. He nodded at Meri. "This was Morcant's table. Now it belongs to us."

"No." She shook her head. "He's coming back for it." She cut her eyes around at the small group, her heart thumping heavily in her chest.

"Meri," Rider breathed.

"She can't help it, my friend. She's a seer." Blake inched his way between the furniture towards her as he encouraged, "Go on. Have a look around. Nothing here will harm you."

Licking her lips, Merideth turned, marveling at the blend of old and new. The shop had been transformed, but she could feel the lingering past. Her eyes falling on Rider, a displeased scowl crinkled his forehead. "You wanted to stay." She left it at that, strolling through the shop.

At the register, she paused. Placing her hand on the counter, she ran it along the old flat top. Her fingers reaching the sales device, she caressed it, as if it were dear to her. "He sat here, too. This was his for many years."

"Yes, Morcant ran M & J's," Blake admitted quietly, trailing after her.

"I knew this was the right place," Rider spat. "Why don't you just tell us where to find him? Stop toying with my girlfriend already."

"She'll find him. She's gifted, despite your desire to hide her talent," Blake replied, his gaze fixed on the girl.

Next to him, Sarah squirmed. "Are they here for us?" she asked covertly.

"They haven't said why they're here. They are looking for Morcant and Judoc," he explained, following along as Meri left the storefront and moved through the door to the back.

"Judoc –" Sarah managed before his hand shot up to stop her, motioning for her to go back to her cleaning.

"We're here to find our sister," Rider huffed.

"Your sister! I thought she was your girlfriend." Blake gasped, indicating Meri as she disappeared down the back stairs, which led to the basement below. Catching up to her at the bottom, he growled, "Ok, tell me who you guys are."

Merideth stood before a large wooden door, petrified at the memories trapped on the other side. "What an evil place," she whispered.

"Yeah, you said that," Blake shouted.

Turning to meet his gaze, she stammered, "You. You've been here a long time, too. You are part of this." Fear gripping her, she brushed past him, shocked by vivid images when they collided for the briefest of moments. At the stairs, she climbed as quickly as she could, panting at the top. Back at their chore, the two girls seemed unaware of the darkness that surrounded them, and yet she sensed they too were part of it.

Behind her, Blake clomped to the top of the stairs, adding fuel to the fire within her chest. On the verge of panic, Meri squealed. Tears on her face, she looked around wildly, as if she were a trapped animal in search of an escape.

"It's ok," Blake soothed as he reached her. His hand firm, he ran his palm over her back, then made his way around to face her. Catching her hand, he squeezed it tightly, pulling her body to stand toe to toe with him. "Just breathe, Merideth. You're safe here."

Still winded, she fought for control. Blinking rapidly, she stemmed the flow of tears. Unable to speak, she focused on the pale blue eyes that bore into hers.

"What are you doing?" Rider demanded loudly.

"She needs to find her center. She's overwhelmed. That's it, Meri." He adjusted his grip on her hand, working her with his fingers. "Tell me why you're here."

"My mother sent us. To find my sister. She gave her away when she was born," Meri explained in short clips.

Drawn to him, she squeezed Blake's hand. "You are turned from the darkness," she whispered.

"Yes. Just relax. I told you, you are safe here." Blake's voice low, their conversation had become quiet, as if it were meant for only the two of them.

His temper rising, Rider interceded. "Her mother and my father had a child together. This Morcant and Judoc were old friends of theirs, and they helped find the baby a home. Or at least that's what my father told us."

"A sister to each of you." Blake smiled. "You are Ezamay's heir."

"Yes." Meri nodded vigorously, her pulse calmer. "My mother is dying, and she asked me to find my sister. She wants to see her before she passes." Pausing, her brown eyes filled with wonder. "You know my mother?"

"Dying," Blake repeated, his brow furrowed. Easing his grip on her, he nodded. "Yes, I know your mother, but you and I have never met as it has been a long time since I have seen May. Or Teddy," he added, glancing at Rider.

"Teddy." Rider winced. "Ok, Blake." He bit his name as if it were a curse. "Mind letting go of my girl and telling us who *you* really are?"

"Not at all." He released her hand, stepping back with a slight bow. "I am Judoc."

"Bullshit." Rider sized him up, as if it were the first time he had seen him. "Judoc is an old man. My father's age, if not more. They were old friends."

"Indeed. I see there are a good many things Thaddeus has neglected to share with you. Why is that, I wonder." Turning on his heel, he called to the girls as he switched off the outside lights and locked the glass entrance. "Would one of you make us some coffee? And then you girls might as well join us." Grinning when Sarah dropped her rag and bounced towards the back, he turned to their guests. "Let's sit and get to know each other. It would seem we have much to share."

"How about you just tell us where Joseline is and we'll be on our way," Rider suggested through clenched teeth.

"Rider," Merideth whispered, considering kicking him. "He's going to help, don't make him regret it."

"Ah, you two." Blake clapped his hands together. "And to see the man you have become." He indicated Rider by opening his palms towards him. "You were only a small boy when I saw you last. An impetuous toddler bouncing about the night we took the child. Seems little has changed, but did you say her name is Joseline? How do you know this?"

"I am not impetuous," Rider denied flatly. "My father has been watching her through a crystal." Digging in his pocket, Rider produced the glass ball, which he held towards their host. Noting that Meri followed the motion intently, he sighed.

"She can't help it, you know," Blake stated flatly as he accepted the trinket. "We have many crystals such as this." He indicated the wall of merchandise. "But this one is very old. A family heirloom. It has watched many of your line." He handed it to Meri instead of back to Rider, who tried to snatch it away from her.

Blake stepped between them, standing up to him. "That does not belong to you. You are hurting her, with your pride and foolish notions."

"We are non-practicing," Rider bit back.

"Nonsense." Blake glanced at the girl, who held the

crystal a few inches from her face. "What do you see, Meri?"

"It's Joseline. I'm sure of it!"

"You see?" He turned to her mate. "She is a witch, and a talented one from the look of it. Her power springs from within her. You should not ask her to hide who and what she is."

"Don't give me that. Power comes from spells and charms. You can not use them as easily as you can," Rider sputtered. "It's all a matter of choice."

Joining them with a round tray of coffee and cups, Sarah gasped, "We're talking about magic? What did I miss?"

"Only Rider, showing his ass." Indicating the sitting area, Blake added, "Shall we?"

Grasping Merideth's arm, Rider roughly guided her towards the chairs. Glaring at her new toy, he didn't try to take it again. She would give it to him later if he asked, so why make a fuss now? Taking two chairs next to each other, a small table separating them, he indicated for her to sit.

Watching them together, Blake chuckled, then noticed that Karen had remained at her post. Calling, he motioned to her, "Take a break. Come and visit with us."

Reluctantly leaving her stack of books, she lamented, "I wanted to finish that shelf. We have so much to do before I leave."

Sarah rolled her eyes, still miffed her friend intended to abandon her. "We'll get it done. Right now, I'm curious about this tiny crystal ball. I tried some of them when we got our shipment, but they don't work. I figured they were a hoax." She laughed anxiously. "I'm still new to the whole witch thing."

"Me too," Meri commiserated, then took her chair, careful not to touch the cursed table a few feet away. Closing her palm around the glass sphere, she squeezed it, then hunted in her purse for a handkerchief. Wrapping it, she tucked it into a pocket inside the bag and zipped the top. Placing her hands on her knees, she sat up straight and grinned.

Rider's gut twisted at her joy. "Oh, Meri." Turning to Blake, he demanded, "How are you and Judoc the same person, and why are you calling yourself Blake? And why –"

"Is that really what you want to know?" The other man's lips curled, his amusement evident.

"There's lots I want to know, dammit!" Rider shouted back.

"Calm down, Boo. I'm sure we're going to learn more than we could have imagined. Are you guys a coven? Is Blake the magister?"

Rider gaped at her excitement. "We're non-practicing," he stated hoarsely.

Shaking his head, Blake poured coffee, offering the first cup to Meri. "We aren't much of a coven these days with only the three of us." Cutting his eyes over at Rider, he added, "We've downsized. Morcant was the magister, but with him gone, I'll be stepping into that role."

"We're recruiting," Sarah chimed in, her red locks shimmering as she shook them with excitement.

"We aren't here for all that," Rider reminded them. "We are here to locate one wayward sister and return her to her mother. Then we go back to NOLA and normal life."

Ignoring everything he had said, Blake continued. "I will do my best to help you locate your missing sibling, but we will need some help. Morcant and I passed her to another friend, who placed her with a family. I didn't even know her name until today."

"What if we can't find her?" Meri's smile faded at the thought of failing their mission.

"You see her in the glass. I believe that means that she's alive and well, and likely we will locate her," he reassured.

"How does she see into the glass?" Sarah persisted. "I really am curious how it works."

"May I?" Blake held his hand towards Meri, indicating he wanted to hold the object of their discussion.

Placing her mug on the small table between her and Rider, Meri avoided looking at her mate. She could feel his anger but was powerless in that regard. Opening her bag, she retrieved the sphere, careful when she unwrapped it before presenting it to him. "Rider's father gave it to me."

"He said she was a seer, too. What does that mean, exactly?" Rider sounded calmer, a welcome surprise.

"A seer has vision beyond the here and now. They use objects and sometimes people to access what you might call memories," Blake explained. "They can also be of future events or might be things that do not ever happen."

"But how does she make the ball show her things?" Karen chimed in. "Is it a spell?"

"No, it's more like a union between them. You can't force the crystal to show you anything. It shows you what it will, not what you desire. Being a seer is a special gift, not suited for everyone. It's one of the gifts non-natural born witches are very unlikely to possess." He turned the ball in his hand a few times. "Even full blood, I can't force it. I see nothing." Handing it back to her, he picked up his mug and sat back in his chair. "I have answered many of your questions. Answer some of mine."

Rider glared at him. "What do you want to know?"

"How did the two of you become a couple? I thought your families were sworn enemies."

"Merideth mended the rift between us a couple of years ago. Her mother put her up to it," Rider divulged. "I helped at my father's request."

"Interesting. And how is it you consider yourselves non-practicing? Surely you realize I do not believe in this." Blake took a noisy sip. "I have known others who have tried. Most failed and miserably."

Glancing at Merideth, Rider inhaled deeply. "We decided it was better if we left magic aside. Pretty much set our families aside. Things got pretty ugly, and we don't need that in our lives."

Blake's jaw dropped, as if he intended to speak. An instant later, he clamped it shut, cutting his eyes over to the girl. Rubbing at his chin with his free hand, he grimaced. "Man, it's been a long day. Maybe we should call it a night. We'll see if we can pick up Joseline's trail tomorrow."

"I guess we can do that," Rider agreed reluctantly. "We'll get a hotel and meet you back here in the morning."

"Nonsense!" Sarah got to her feet to collect their cups. "We have a mansion and it's just the three of us."

"It's not really a mansion," Blake disagreed, shaking his head. "But you are welcome to stay with us if you like."

Rider glanced at Merideth. Judging from the smile on her face, he wouldn't have any luck convincing her of anything else.

SEVEN

Perspective

BLAKE and the girls climbed inside his sporty red Camaro. Tucked in the back seat, Karen rested half turned in her seat.

"You didn't have much to say to our visitors," Blake observed. Pulling the car into the street, he watched his rearview mirror to see that Rider easily followed. "What do you make of them?"

"Well, they are an odd couple," she replied. Squirming slightly, she sighed. "I'm sorry if I haven't been myself lately. It's just that since I announced I was going home after graduation, I've felt like more of a third wheel than usual."

"Don't be so hard on yourself," Blake commanded. "I know Sarah's taking it hard, but you have to do what's right for you. We'll get by." He cut his eyes over at his girlfriend, giving her a crooked grin. "What do you think of them?"

"I think her ability to see things is amazing. Madam Demore is a seer as well, isn't she?" Sarah's mind leapt to their visit with the older woman over a year ago, in the midst of her being transformed into Brenna. "I'm glad the madam was wrong about me. Or that my perspective on what she said was incorrect. Gees, I haven't thought about those dark times in ages."

"I'm glad it doesn't bother you these days. She wasn't wrong, really. The old Sarah is long gone, and that could be defined as death. Don't you think so, Karen?" He flicked his gaze to look at her in the mirror.

"What? Sorry, I wasn't listening." Shaking her ebony locks, Karen tried to focus.

"Never mind, it doesn't matter," Sarah huffed. "What does matter is finding a way to get them to join the coven."

"I thought they said they were from New Orleans," Karen pointed out crisply. "That's not really going to work if we – I mean you…" her voice trailed away at the blunder.

"Until we have dealt with their sister, we have time to convince them," Blake pointed out. "In the meantime, we need to treat them well."

"Yeah, like telling Rider he's showing his ass." Sarah cackled. "I'm sure he really appreciated that. But I'm glad you agree on adding them to our number. I don't really know them, but I like what I see. Even if Rider's an ass."

Blake gripped the wheel tightly, his jaw tight. "He was, dammit. And his father is a real jerk. If it hadn't been May who asked, I wouldn't be involved in any of this now."

"Is that why you were so tender with Merideth?" Karen asked cautiously while staring at the back of

Blake's seat. "You sure got her boyfriend riled up, holding her hand and all."

"I was helping her," Blake explained with a sputter. "Telling her she can't use her powers is like telling cats they aren't allowed to hunt. It goes against their instincts and will only lead to problems."

"Maybe she'll stay with us, even if he doesn't," Sarah suggested thoughtfully.

"Perhaps." Blake nodded at the idea of it. "That is, if she can separate herself from him."

"He did appear a bit controlling," Karen observed.

"Indeed." Blake made a turn, falling into silence as he considered what it would take to secure Ezamay's daughter as a member of their newish coven.

In the car behind them, Merideth leaned against her door. Her head on the glass, she put as much distance as possible between the two of them. Rider drove, his gaze fixed on the taillights leading them to their accommodations, at least for the night. "If we don't find her tomorrow, I'm going to check us into a hotel. We don't want to impose."

Meri shook her head, not bothering to reply. Closing her eyes, she thought about the small sphere tucked inside her bag. The smooth leather gripped firmly in her lap, she didn't dare open it to remove her new crystal for fear Rider would find a way to take it from her. She knew he wanted it. Or didn't want her to have it, to be more precise.

"That guy sure is flashy," Rider continued. His eyes darting to her purse, he noted how closely she held onto it and considered how he might ask for his father's crystal. If she wasn't willing to give it to him, it would only make her more afraid. Putting his eyes back on the road, he decided it might be better to find a way to sneak it from her.

Meri seemed to suspect his plan, adjusting her grip. "Please don't take it from me."

His heart stopped. He could argue his case from several points. Deciding on the one he liked best, he replied calmly, "Why do you need it? I shouldn't have to tell you that getting involved with this group is a bad idea."

"We're already involved," she pointed out calmly, then asked, "Don't you feel the energy here?"

Rider didn't care about energy. He wanted to go home and return their lives to normal. "We're here on a mission, Boo. Let's focus on getting to Joseline and taking her back to Virginia while there's still time. Once that chore is done, we'll be able to return to our lives. *Our* home."

Meri inhaled deeply, returning her focus to the street whizzing by. In her heart, she couldn't see how that would happen. Her eyes had been opened. All Blake had to do was hold her hand. She had never spent time in the company of those who used the craft. She felt intrigued, drawn to the mysterious power that fueled her intuition. The strange gift that enabled her to see her lost sister within a small ball of glass. She had tried to tell him about it, but Rider didn't want to hear. Knowing this rift existed between them saddened her, and she feared that her life with him would soon come to an end, despite his profession of love and dreams for their future.

Pulling up in front of the house, Rider suggested firmly, "Don't divulge more than you have to. I don't trust Blake, and I fear very deeply that we are in over our heads."

Inside the other car, Blake delivered a similar warning to the girls. "Take them in and give them a room. We'll make dinner and see what info we can glean from them. But be careful. We don't want to tell them anything until we are ready."

"Ready for what?" Sarah asked, not moving.

"I have some things I need to find out before we trust them with everything, that's all," Blake clarified. Opening his door, he stepped out, motioning for Rider and Merideth to come and join them inside.

Hours later, Rider stared at the ceiling of their room. Arms folded behind his head, he listened to the silence. "Thank God," he muttered. Up until a few minutes ago, he had the distinct pleasure of overhearing a very noisy fuck session, and it hadn't been his.

Dinner had turned out to be an extended game of cat and mouse. Rider would ask questions that Blake would sidestep. Then Blake would ask questions that Rider would avoid with equal skill. Flashy smiles hid their intentions, leaving much said and little gained. The girls had talked, though, so he hoped that Meri had at least learned something useful.

Merideth must have been exhausted. She had flat refused his advances and fell asleep as soon as she curled beneath the covers. To make matters worse, she had hidden his father's crystal inside her pillow. Not just under it. She had shoved it to the bottom, where he could stare at the lump of it next to his. The only way to steal it from her would be to take the entire pillow and fish it out. *Too bad I'm not as skilled at the craft as good old Blake. I could just zap it out of there if I were,* he mused.

"Clever girl," he observed, shifting to watch her shoulder rise and fall as she breathed. Her back to him, forlorn sorrow filled his gut. Turning to match her, he trailed gentle fingers down her bare skin. "God, how I love you, Meri. It was a stupid way to propose."

He should have planned an elegant evening. Or an exciting adventure with a ring at the end. Anything would have been better than the terrified push he had given her yesterday. "I'll make it up to you. I promise," he whispered. Closing his eyes, he drifted off to a fitful sleep.

EIGHT

Demore She Knows

MERIDETH ARRIVED in the kitchen the following morning like a breath of fresh air. Her hair swept into a loose bun, she fussed with it as she entered, her brown eyes bright with anticipation. "What can I do to help?"

"Good morning, Sunshine," Blake complimented freely from his seat at the table, noting her mate stumbling in behind her. Disheveled, the pair contrasted perfectly. "Sleep well?" he added, addressing her mate.

"No," Rider groaned, giving the other man a dark glare, then sharing it with Sarah at the stove. When he made it to Karen next to her, their friend giggled.

"Don't blame me," the tall brunet teased. "I was alone in my room. All night."

Turning to Meri, she added, "Thanks for the offer, but you are our guest. Have a seat and we'll have breakfast ready shortly."

Accepting a cup of coffee from Sarah, Meri did as instructed. Securing a chair next to Blake, she snuggled closer to him, whispering, "Good morning yourself."

"Where's the crystal?" he covertly replied.

"In my pocket." She beamed, pleased at its closeness.

"Nice. Keep it safe, love."

Sitting on the other side of his girlfriend, Rider scowled at the pair. Slurping loudly from his own cup of brew, he demanded bluntly, "Any chance we can get some real intel today?"

Running his fingers over the thin goatee surrounding his mouth, Blake grinned. "I may have a bit to share. You don't seem to be much of a morning person."

"My mornings are fine," Rider snapped. "I'm tired of the run around."

Placing plates of eggs, sausage and bacon on the table, the girls joined them, Sarah observing, "You do seem a little grumpy, Rider. Maybe you should have slept in."

Accepting the food, Rider cut his eyes around at the group. He'd had a few sleepless hours to think things over and was in no mood for further games. "You'd like that, wouldn't you," he growled.

Silence fell over the group. Serving themselves, they ate, tension filling the small space.

"What, no snappy comeback, Judoc?" he goaded, glaring at Blake across Meri's plate.

"I'm not sure what you mean," Blake huffed. "And don't call me that. I have not answered to that name in years."

"I bet. How many years?" Rider pushed his plate back, too pissed for food. "I've been doing some think-ing, see? I want to know exactly how you can be a friend of my father, who is damn near sixty, and yet you don't look a day over thirty."

"Well, I wouldn't say I look that young," Blake mocked. "Thirty-five, maybe." He sipped a glass of orange juice loudly, throwing fuel on the flames.

"That tears it!" Rider slapped the table with an open palm, bouncing the dishes and causing the group to jump. "Why do you hate me? I've done nothing to you, damn it. We just met, for fuck's sake."

Studying him, Blake pursed his lips. Placing his glass calmly on the table, he inhaled deeply, then released the breath slowly. "I do not know my exact age. Suffice it to say, better than a century plus a dime." He grinned coyly. "The best part is, your father had a family when I was a child. I grew up with them. Two boys and three girls. He is even older than I am, and quite the breeder." He chuckled, seeming to enjoy tearing his old friend down.

"My father is not a breeder!" Rider denied flatly. "And how could he or you be that old?"

"We're witches. The purer the blood, the longer we live." Pushing back his own plate, Blake placed his elbows on the table and folded his hands before him.

"That's bullshit," Rider accused. "Anyone can be a witch. With the proper motivation and training, any fool off the street can cast."

"I'm not talking about casting," Blake stated more calmly. Tapping his lips with the edges of his fingers, he said more gently. "I have many things I could share with you, but they are painful for me. You must forgive me if I impart my anger towards him to you."

"You mean the tuath," Meri suggested gently.

"Yes. You have heard of our line, then," Blake praised.

"Only in passing. We were told to visit one in New Orleans while on our quest."

"Visit one," Blake repeated, staring at her. "Then you really don't know."

"Oh, man," Rider grumbled, tussling his hair. "Look, say what you gotta say. We need the truth—and no, my father was never good at telling it. When he speaks, you are better off not taking him at his word. Is he over a century old? Doubtful. Did he have a family he forgot to mention? In light of Joseline, the jury is still out on that one."

"Is it true?" Meri asked, her voice unsteady. "If Teddy is ancient, does that mean my mother is as well?" The thought of more secret siblings disturbed her deeply.

"Your mother is older than me, but not by much," Blake explained. Speaking to the girl made his sharing easier, and he focused on her. "She and I were very good friends. I know that she would have helped me if she could have."

"Do you believe this?" Rider asked, addressing the two girls across from him.

"Well, we did almost die a year ago," Sarah shared, toying with her fork.

"Blake's mother saved us," Karen added. "She's an antique old crone. So, yeah. You could say that we believe him."

Reaching for his plate, Rider began shoveling in the food. Following his lead, the group returned to their meals, the level of tension dropping as his anger ebbed. When he had finished, he tried again. "Ok, Blake. My father had a family long ago. So where are they now?"

"That is not my story to tell." Blake held his tone in check, making the effort to keep their heads cool.

Tears filled Meri's eyes. "Do my parents have other children as well? Please, Blake. You have to tell me. Not knowing is torture."

"I need a smoke." Blake stood, leaving them at the table to search for his pack.

Rising, Sarah and Karen cleared the dishes in his absence. When he returned, he dropped the box and an ashtray on the table. Taking a long drag, he eyed the couple still seated, patiently waiting. Taking one of the chairs across from them, he coughed into his fist to clear his throat.

"I'm going to tell you only what you must know. Your parents' past is theirs to share, so if you want details other than that, you will speak to them." He laid out the rules firmly, waiting for the couple to agree before he continued.

"I've had my own struggles. Dark times, some of which Teddy was a part of," Blake supplied.

"Is that why you despise him so?" Rider interrupted.

"Perhaps." Blake shrugged. "It took me to a dark place. One I spent many years trapped within. It was only recently that I found my way out."

"So you changed your name," Meri surmised.

"Yes. Dropping my old moniker became my signal to the world that I had found peace with the past." He took a long drag, then crushed out the butt, dropping it next to the others in the dish. "Morcant is still very much a part of that darkness."

"Yes," Meri hissed in agreement. She had seen

shadows of it when she touched his table and shuddered at the thought of it.

"He would like nothing more than to destroy me. Us." Blake indicated the two girls behind him. "He damn sure tried last year, and as Karen said, he would have succeeded, if my mother hadn't taken my side...for once."

"Ok, so your family has drama," Rider teased.

"We all do," Meri clipped, squirming next to him.

"Yeah, we all do," Blake echoed. "Right now, the drama we need to deal with is Joseline. The problem is, she was supposed to have been placed in secret. That's where Madam Demore comes in."

Rising for fresh coffee, Blake filled his cup, his gaze on the past. Leaning against the counter, he sighed. "Before the child was born, Teddy came to ask me if I would hide it for them. Well, Morcant and I. I'm not sure if Ezamay knew then what he was planning, but after the birth, they both returned, bringing us the child. She couldn't have been more than a few hours old. May was in obvious pain."

Meri sniffed, fresh tears smearing her mascara. "My poor mother. How hard it must have been."

Retaking his seat, Blake reached for her hand, folding her fingers between his. "May is a strong woman. She always has been. She knew their daughter wouldn't be safe with the feud between their families. She asked me to hide her infant and keep her safe."

"Thank you." Meri swiped her drops of sadness. "She was right to trust you."

"Well, I don't know about that." He dropped her digits and leaned back in his chair, his eyes flicking between them. "Madam Demore was to hide her, even from us. She was to place her with a human family. No magic. If Thad found her, I'm concerned the proper precautions weren't followed after all."

"But you said she was safe," Rider pointed out. "And the feud is ended."

"Why would you choose a human family?" Meri asked. "If she's a witch, wouldn't she need a magical family who would understand her?" The question revealed her doubts about the way she had been raised, in the dark about her true nature and abilities. "I'm not saying what my mother did was wrong, not telling me," she gushed. "But in hindsight, I regret that I had to find out the way that I did."

"A magical child will discover their power regardless of how they are brought up." Blake glanced at Sarah. "Besides, it was Demore's suggestion that the extra precautions be taken. She foresaw that Joseline's path would affect many lives. We feared this would mean an all-out war between the families if she were discovered. In the end, we agreed it would be the best path to take."

"I guess this means we need to visit with this Madam Demore," Merideth surmised with a sigh. "Damn. Here I thought we were close to finding her."

"We are close," Blake reassured. "Another day or two, and you should have your secret sister. Then you can take her home, if she is willing to go."

"You think she may not be?" Meri gasped. "What if she refuses?"

"She won't refuse." Rider dropped his arm across her shoulders, considering the possibility. "But that does bring up another problem. What if she hasn't discovered her magic?"

The group exchanged glances, each weighing the implications. Finally, Blake stated, "Let's visit with Demore before we worry about that. If we have to, we'll keep that piece of information to ourselves."

NINE

Never to Speak

GATHERING their jackets against the cool morning, Sarah suggested, "Karen and I'll take the bus to the shop. We have tons more work to do. Besides, we don't all need to go see Madam Demore."

"You're just afraid of what she might tell you," Blake accused with a laugh. Seeing his girlfriend did not appear amused, he pulled the keys to his car from his pocket. "No need for the bus, Babe. Just don't wreck it. I'll ride with these two in theirs." He indicated their visitors with a thumb.

"Oh yeah?" Rider teased. "Who said you could?"

"Oh, Rider." Meri punched him in the arm. "When will you two men get along?"

Blake squinted at his nemesis, considering that they never would. "You do want to find Joseline," he reminded gently.

"Yes, so let's go," Rider agreed. Climbing behind the wheel, he watched Merideth give up her seat to the other man. "You're taking the back, Boo?"

"He's bigger, he should get the roomy front," she explained with a grin. "Besides, it'll be good for you to practice speaking without spitting like a pair of tomcats." Through the front glass, she noticed Sarah putting food in a bowl, a cat rubbing her leg. "Oh, what a pretty kitty!" A fluffy yellow and black patchwork of fur covered the slender body.

"That's Caly," Blake informed her as he slid into his seat. Adjusting his safety belt, he grinned. "She's Sarah's cat. We've had her a few years."

"She's quite beautiful," Meri breathed. "We don't have any pets."

"Thank goodness," Rider chimed in. "They'd be starving right now. Where to?"

Pulling out his phone, Blake loaded the directions and started the quest. "You can follow google, right?"

"I'm not an idiot," Rider shot back.

"Boys, no spitting. Remember?" Meri rebuked them firmly.

Opting for silence, Rider followed the mechanical voice, arriving at Demore's place a short time later. Climbing out, the trio entered the shop and paused for their eyes to adjust to the dim décor.

"I guess she doesn't believe in lights." Rider grimaced as he scanned the room. Candles spotted the walls and tabletops, providing a meager amount of dancing light.

"She must have known we were coming," Blake surmised.

"Of course, I knew." Madam Demore made her entrance, pushing her curtain of beads aside. At only five foot, the medium made up for her stature with her formidable presence. "Judoc Korrigan, at my door again. And you have brought more visitors!"

"We're not really visitors," Rider explained, offering the old woman his hand. "We're looking for someone."

"Indeed," the shopkeeper breathed. His digits wrapped in hers, she grinned. "An old witch has found his way home."

"I – I'm not an old witch," Rider stammered, withdrawing his appendage. "I'm non-practicing," he added for good measure.

"And yet you are here," she pushed. Raising one of her wrinkled palms, she indicated a few straight-backed chairs circled around a table. In the center stood a larger version of Merideth's crystal.

"How quaint," Rider observed, moving to take a seat. "This place couldn't be more cliché if you tried."

"This is Thaddeus Bradshaw's son," Blake informed their host as if it were an apology.

"Indeed. The resemblance is striking, and he looks like him, too!" Her eyes sparkled as she took her chair on the backside of the flat surface. "And who might you be?" she asked, turning her attention to Merideth.

"I'm Ezamay's daughter. Merideth Monroe." Meri smiled meekly, unsure what to think of their extraordinary host. "Your crystal is much larger than mine." Pulling it from her pocket, she held up her small glass sphere.

"Another seer," Demore whispered. "We are so few and far between."

"My father is a seer," Blake reminded her sharply.

"Thad Bradshaw has a shadow of talent, at best,"

Demore countered. "Using a family crystal to view loved ones does not a seer make."

"Ok, so he's a fraud. Tell me something new. Where we might find our sister, perhaps?" Rider glared at the old woman, unimpressed with what he had seen so far.

"Please," Blake added, giving the other man a sharp glare. "I swear, you have the worst manners."

"Oh, brother. Boys." Meri sighed, rolling her eyes as she returned her crystal to her pocket.

Folding her hands in her lap, Madam Demore waited. When the trio had settled into their seats and were quiet, she began. "You seek that which is hidden."

"Because you hid it." Rider shrugged. "Or so we are told."

"Yes, I did aid in the secrecy which has made you so bitter." Her hand popped up, her flat palm signaling he need not comment. "I understand the pain her discovery has brought you. The fear that lingers within our heart."

Rider's lips formed a stiff, straight line at his refusal to be baited. Watching him from the side, Meri slid her hand over his leg, grasping his fingers. Squeezing, she silently lent him her support.

"And Ezamay's heir! How befitting that you should seek this secret sister together!" Madam Demore appeared pleased. "We agreed never to speak of the child, but what harm could come from a little peek?" Gazing into the glass before her, her smile grew strained. "Oh, my. It would appear I hid her so well, her return to me has escaped my attention."

"You know who she is?" Meri asked hoarsely.

"I'm afraid I do. She has provided the illumination for our gathering." Her meaning unclear, she used extended digits to indicate the flame-kissed walls. "Joseline is the candle maker. She is the sibling you seek."

"The candle maker," Blake growled. "She's *that* Joseline?"

"You're familiar with her as well?" Meri asked in surprise.

"I'm afraid so. She supplied M & J's before Morcant went to –" he stopped cold, omitting the word prison. Swallowing, he added, "I let her go when I took over the shop. But I also had no idea. I guess your precautions were better than I thought," he added tartly. "How did Teddy see her then?"

"Family crystal," Madam Demore explained. "As a parent, he gained access through the heirloom. Enough to watch, but my enchantments remain strong. She is safe from those who might wish to harm her."

"We do not have any such plans," Meri squealed. "We need to speak with her. My mother is waiting for our return!"

Madam Demore's face twisted into a grimace. "That would be unwise. Although I do not see happiness in Joseline's life, I fear the outcome of your meeting would not improve that fact."

"She's unhappy? Why?" Rider demanded.

"It is not for me to say." Demore shrugged. "Nor is it for you to hear. Go and introduce yourselves if you must; but be warned…" She waggled a finger at them, "darkness follows the child of Thaddeus and Ezamay. They were cautioned of the destruction she would bring before her conception and again at her birth."

"You're saying my sister is cursed," Meri snapped, anger staining her cheeks a bright pink.

"She is unfortunate to carry such darkness, but I see your minds are set and no threats will dissuade you. Go then, leave an old woman in peace." Rising, Madam Demore shuffled to her beaded exit, plunging through it without so much as a backwards glance.

"Wow!" Meri panted. "She's quite forceful in her readings." She briefly pondered what it might be like to tell fortunes, only to have them ignored.

"Great!" Rider sang, obviously not pleased at the hasty departure. "Where to next, chief?"

"That's easy." Blake dodged the remark. Getting to his feet, he headed for the door. "Joseline is the owner of The Broken Match Candle Shop."

TEN

Whether the Storm

"I'VE GOT the boxes packed and labeled, Sis." Hubert Tipton joined Joseline in her tiny office. "Do we have enough to cover the shipping?"

"We have to," she lamented. Pulling her glasses down, she pressed on her closed eyelids. "They've already been paid for. If we don't ship, we just piss them off."

"I'll call for a pickup then," he offered. Noting her hunched frame, he ran his hand firmly over her back. "I know things are hard, but they'll get better, Jos."

"Yeah, if the comeback can happen fast enough," she agreed. The pandemic had hit them hard, the shutdown cutting off their sales like a light switch. "If it weren't for those online orders, we'd already be sunk."

Getting to her feet, she pushed her glasses back up her nose and into position. "Go on, and I'll start today's batch of wax. I saw that M & J were cleaning out their shop. I'm still hoping Blake will decide to give us an order."

"I thought he quit us. Said they were going in a 'new

direction' or some shit like that." He mocked their client, providing air quotes as he imitated Blake's voice.

"Yeah, well, after all these months, I'm hoping he changed his mind. They were one of our biggest clients," she reminded him as she scooped the bills she had been sorting into a pile. "Besides, someone was shot over there, and his brother went to prison. No matter how bad it is here, I thank God every day I'm not over there, in his shoes."

"Think that's why they gave it that name?" Bert shoved his hands in his pockets. "I'm not sure it will change their outlook. People still know what happened."

"Hard to say." She gave her little brother a grin. "We still have each other and that's good enough for me. Get on that pickup and I'll get the burner's going."

Joseline hadn't even gotten her wax hot when Hubert burst into the back. "You're not going to believe who's here," he panted.

"Who?" She grinned at his enthusiasm, aware it could be anyone.

"Blake Korrigan. And he's got two people with him. I heard he took on new partners. I bet that's them!" Almost giddy, he reached over and cut off her heat. "You can do all this later, Sis. Come out front and haggle."

"Ok, I'm coming. Let me get this smock off." Pulling the tie in the back, she released the glorified apron. Hardly more than a couple of towels strung together, she had worn the article every time she dipped for years, almost thinking of it as her lucky rags. Leaving it across her stool, she smoothed her blouse and released her bun, then ran her fingers through her long wavey hair.

"Well, Blake. What can I do for you?" She greeted

him with a large grin. Giving Rider a cursory glance, she noted her old client had chosen well. She froze when she came to Merideth. "What the hell is going on?" she snapped. "Is this some kind of joke? A prank, Blake?" She pivoted, facing her target squarely.

"Maybe I should have waited in the car," Meri offered. She had seen the girl in her crystal and knew the resemblance was striking.

"Too late now," Rider observed with a low whistle.

"Joseline, these are friends of mine. This is Rider and Merideth –"

"Friends?" Jos cut him off. "Very funny. How long did you have to look before you found my double? As if dropping my business wasn't enough." She turned on her heel, stomping towards the back.

Blake caught her arm. "We aren't finished talking to you," he bit through clenched teeth. Holding her firmly, he refused to let her go.

"Hey," Rider interceded. "Let go of her. We didn't come here to fight."

"Then what did you come here for?" Joseline stopped her struggle. Her eyes cut over to the girl. "Are you a friend of Morcant's as well?"

"I don't know him," Meri whispered. "That's not why we're here. My mother is dying; she sent us to find you."

"Your mother," Joseline gasped as Blake released her. "Who the hell is your mother?"

"Oh, shit," Hubert interrupted, leaping to the conclusion of their debate. His eyes wide, he stared at Blake, chewing his bottom lip.

Blake nodded. "Yeah. We've got some explaining to

do, but that needs to happen when you are calmer." He stepped back, giving the girl some room.

"Bullshit," Rider grunted. "We don't have time to mess around here. Ezamay could die any second and we promised to bring our sister home."

"Your sister!" Joseline tossed her honey brown locks. "Look, I don't know who you people are, but you can get the hell out of my shop. I have work to do."

Letting her go this time, Blake took another step back, turning to Hubert. "You don't look surprised."

"I'm not," Bert confessed. "I mean I am. I never would have guessed you had anything to do with it, but yeah. I know she's an imposter. Or adopted. Or whatever you want to call it."

"Imposter," Blake chortled. "Don't tell her that. How did you know?"

"I have some proof. I can show it to her if you want, after she's cooled down a little," Hubert offered.

"That'll be fine," Blake agreed. "We'll be at the shop when she's ready to talk."

"Wait, so we're just going to leave without her?" Rider demanded.

"Oh, you want to take her by force? Sure, asshat. She's in there." Blake pointed at the door to the back.

"We should leave her be." Merideth lifted her chin, taking Blake's side. "We'll talk to her when she comes to us."

"And what if she doesn't come to us?" Rider insisted.

"Then we go back without her. We'll tell Mother that we couldn't locate her, and that will be that." She turned to the door as she spoke, emphasizing her decision.

"Let it go, just like that. Do you realize how disappointed she is going to be?" Rider stomped after her, not ready to give up.

"It has to be Joseline's choice," Meri insisted, the exit closing behind her.

"Don't worry," Hubert assured him. "I'll talk to her. Hang around for a few days and I'll see what I can do."

"Thanks man." Blake offered a nod, clamping Rider on the back and shoving him after the girl.

Climbing into the car, Rider slammed his door, then pivoted to glare at his girlfriend, who had already claimed the back seat. "Why did you give up so easily?"

"I couldn't do it, Rider. She's…broken." Tears spilled over onto her cheeks.

"Broken," he parroted, the car shaking as Blake joined them, closing his portal a bit more gently. "What's that supposed to mean?"

"She's faced hardships," Blake supplied. "Remember? Madam Demore said she wasn't happy with her life."

"She also pointed out that our arrival wouldn't change that," Meri quickly added. "She has this darkness about her. And that other guy…" She shuddered violently. "I'm not sure I want to take her to my mother."

Rider grimaced. "I think you are taking this seer business why too seriously." Cutting Blake an angry scowl, he righted himself in his seat and started the engine.

"Are we going back to the shop?"

"What else can we do?" Blake asked calmly. "Unless you want to pick up some lunch and take it with us for the girls."

"Yeah, lets grab lunch," Rider mocked. Throwing the

car into drive, he spun the tires as he jetted into the street and hunted for a place to stop.

Behind him, Meri wrapped her arms around herself, rocking gently against the upholstered seat. She could tell Rider was angry and she really couldn't blame him. They had come there to talk to Joseline, after all, and they had given up relatively easily, just as he said. But she couldn't convey the foreboding she had felt back in the Broken Match. "That's a clever name," she mumbled aloud.

"What name?" Rider bit, still put out.

"The Broken Match. Somehow, it suits her."

Glancing over his shoulder, Blake soothed, "Don't worry, Meri. We'll get her sorted out. Just give her some time. Maybe her brother will come through for us."

She may have nodded, but Merideth wasn't nearly as confident, and the words of Madam Demore's warning rang in her ears. Laying her head back against the seat, she simply whispered to herself, "I'm more worried whether the storm we have unleashed is going to sink us."

ELEVEN

Kin to Confession

"CANDLES LOOK GOOD, SIS." Hubert sidled up beside Joseline, admiring her work as she positioned the rack for drying.

"Thanks. Sis? Does that mean you changed your mind about the whole silly adoption thing?"

"You're still my sister, even if you were adopted," he offered. Holding his package with both hands, he wriggled his fingers, causing the brown envelope to crinkle. He had confronted Joseline after the others left, but she stubbornly refused to listen, so he had gone home to retrieve the precious papers. "I'm glad you've calmed down while I was gone."

"That your proof?" She raised her chin to indicate her intention.

"Yeah. This is it."

"What if I don't want to see it?" She cut her eyes up to stare at him.

"What do you mean you don't want to see it?" He met her cool gaze, incredulous.

"What if I don't want to know?" She dropped her hands to her sides, feeling for the towels that hung there. Wiping them crisply, she grunted. "What if I'm happy with the way things are?"

"You aren't happy, Sis. We both know that." He squirmed, not ready to force her to see the truth. He knew Joseline better than anyone, and it hurt him to see her so miserable.

She turned her back on him. "How would you know how I feel?"

"Because you're my sister. I see how hard you work. Things haven't been good for you in a long time. Then Morc got popped, and it just went downhill from there."

"What does Morcant have to do with this?" She swung around to face him, hands on her hips.

"Come on, Sis. I know you two were…" he swallowed, "close."

"We weren't *that* kind of close." She laughed, his misunderstanding lightening her spirits. "But we were good friends. I've missed him. And the strain of losing the shop is a burden, I agree."

"We haven't lost it yet," he countered, bending the envelope between his palms.

"Ok, so start slow. If I say stop, you let it go and don't ever mention today or those people again. Agreed?" She stepped towards him, pointing at the plain brown wrapper. "What's in here?"

"Well, you remember the Christmas surprise for Mom and Dad? The ancestry thing?"

"Yeah, what about it?"

"I lied. They never called to say our samples had been destroyed." He offered her the package.

Her jaw dropped, Joseline considered his words. "They processed our samples?"

"Yes," he clipped.

"And you lied about the results?" she accused. "Why would you do that?"

"Because…" he swallowed, his eyes growing misty. "You're not my sister. When I got the results in the mail, I was so excited. Until I opened them. When I saw that we were no relation, and you had no relatives listed, I panicked. I shoved it all in a drawer and told you to forget it."

Seeing the pain in his eyes, Joseline blinked back tears. "It's real?"

"Yeah, Sis." He waited for her to take the proof, his hand trembling. When she didn't move to do so, he opened the flap and removed the thin sheaf of papers. Holding them out to her he observed, "You will always be my sister, no matter what this says."

Accepting the pages, she glared at the top one. Fumbling, she placed her glasses on her face, then blinked at the page. Turning them slowly, one by one, she ingested the results. "I see," she finally whispered. "Did you tell Mom and Dad about this? It could be a mistake. Maybe I was switched at birth. I mean, they have that picture of the day they brought me home hanging in the living room."

"I didn't tell anyone. I guess I simply pretended it away until today." He shook his head. "I don't think being the wrong baby makes it any better."

"Yeah, me either." She shook her head. "Well, I guess I need to decide what to do. I may go home and sleep on it. Go over to M & J's tomorrow."

"I'll go with you, if you want," he offered.

"I'm not sure they will want you there. This is going to be hard. They said their mother is dying." She sniffed. "I guess that means my mother is dying. It also means that's the only reason they are here."

"I'm not letting you go alone," he informed her curtly. "Someone needs to have your back over there."

"Thanks, Bert. Out of everyone, I know you are always there for me." Her chin quivering, she added, "Maybe we should go now."

"Why now?" He pulled her into a strong hug. "You said you wanted to sleep on it."

"I did. But I'm afraid I'll change my mind. I'm good at that, you know. Hiding things. Pretending I live in the world I want rather than living in the one I have."

Bert squeezed, not sure how to respond to that. "It's ok, Sis. We can go now if you want. You close up the shop and I'll get my car."

"Sure thing," she called after him. Stuffing the pages back in the envelope, she dropped them on her desk as she retrieved her keys and oversized bag, wondering if things could possibly get any worse. Staring at the envelope, she snatched it up, shoving it in her bag as she exited the front and locked the door.

Pulling into the parking lot of the magic shop a short time later, Joseline scowled at the new sign. "Why'd they have to give it such a cutesy name?"

"Because they wanted to?" Hubert laughed. "Come on. I see lights inside, so I'm sure they're still here."

"Yes, that's Blake's pussy-mobile." She pointed out the Camaro. "I'm sure they're here."

Not bothering to knock, Joseline pulled on the handle,

a gentle tug at first to test it, then a hard yank when it opened. Inside, she hesitated, her eyes swinging the full arch. "Everything's changed," she whispered, pain twisting her gut. Morcant's shop was gone.

The group of friends were seated around the familiar table as they entered, but silence fell over the group when Hubert rang the bell a second time. "Hey guys," he called, waving at them. "I got her." He placed his hand on her back, guiding Jos towards the circle of chairs.

Still taking in the view, she clipped, "I love what you've done with the place."

"I doubt that," Blake countered, seeing her disappointed features. "I didn't realize you frequented the store."

"I've been over a few times," Joseline revealed quietly.

On her feet, Meri stepped up to look her older sibling in the eye. Searching the mahogany orbs that matched her own, she waited for Joseline to speak.

"I'm sorry I threw such a fit," their guest began timidly. "I've come to talk. I'm ready. Well, as ready as I'll ever be."

Bouncing slightly, Merideth resisted the urge to yank her into a hug. "So are we," she agreed. "Have a seat. Would you like some coffee?"

"I'll make more, and she can have my seat," Sarah offered graciously.

"Thanks." Jos sank into the comfortable cushions. Opening her bag, she pulled out her brother's proof. "I think we should start with this," she suggested, removing the sheets and spreading them over the table.

"What's all that?" Blake asked, sitting up to take note.

"This was the surprise Hubert and I had planned for our parents a couple of years ago," she explained.

"Christmas 2019," Bert added, taking an empty chair across from her. "Jos and I were going to surprise Mom and Dad with a family tree."

"Only, the surprise was on us," Joseline added, tapping the pages. "When he got the results, he told me that our samples were destroyed so I wouldn't find out." She cut her eyes slowly over at Meri, then to Rider. "But I've always felt out of place with my family. I should have known I didn't really belong to them."

"Why would you hide it?" Rider demanded, bowing up at Bert.

"Hey, man, I didn't know what to think," he shot back. "Sure, she could have been adopted, but what if she had been switched at birth? Can you imagine the pain that would have caused our parents?"

"Let's not argue, ok?" Meri interceded.

His face solemn, Bert sighed. "I've had to carry this burden for two long years. I couldn't tell anyone."

"It's out now," Meri soothed, still not sure what she thought of the younger man. "You don't have to shoulder it alone anymore."

Sarah returned with their coffee, serving everyone a fresh cup. "Wow, the way you described it, I thought this conversation was going to be a mess. You all seem so calm."

"Well, I did have all day to cool off," Joseline pointed out, accepting her mug. As their fingers brushed, she jumped, almost spilling the dark liquid. "Oh, shit! Sorry." Sitting it on the table, she pushed her pages to the side. "How clumsy of me."

Blake blinked rapidly, watching her awkwardness. "Hubert, thank you for helping us out, man. Is there anything we can get for you before you go?"

"Go?" Bert stammered, sipping noisily. "I'm not leaving. She's my sister, too."

"Well, technically, she's not, and we need to talk. Privately," Blake insisted. Getting to his feet, he towered over the smaller man.

"My brother stays," Joseline interrupted. "I rode over with him."

"Fine, we'll drop you at home later. Or back at your shop if you prefer," Blake pushed.

"I'm not leaving." Bert appeared cool. "Anything you have to say to her, I'm perfectly capable of sharing."

"Just let him stay," Rider suggested. "Come on, man."

His eyes sweeping the circle, Blake shrugged. "Fine." Perching on the edge of his chair, he lightly caressed his lips with the tips of his fingers, then plunged in. "Fine. You see this?" He spread his hands wide. "This is a magic shop. That's why it's called Spellbound. We –" he indicated the circle with a sweeping motion "—are a coven. Yes, of witches." He could see Bert's pupils grow wider. He pressed his palms to his chest. "Surprising, isn't it? I'm a witch." He held them out towards Meri. "She's a witch." He indicated Rider with a chuckle. "Even he's a witch. Non-practicing if you believe what he says."

"What's your point?" Bert barked, sitting up straighter in his chair.

"My point, my dear boy, is that she is a witch, too." Blake thrust his hands towards Joseline. "And I don't think you really want to be here for what happens next."

His breath rasping, Hubert leapt to his feet. "I don't care what you call yourselves, if you harm one hair –"

"Oh, for Christ's sake, Bert. Sit down," Joseline commanded sharply. "They aren't going to hurt me." Her bottom lip trembled. "They're going to out me."

"Out you?" Burt gasped, lost for a moment. "They're going to expose your secret?"

"Not that secret." Joseline laughed. "The one I thought I had hidden from everyone." The one that had stood her apart and only left her in pain. "I thought Morcant was the only one who knew."

"My brother spoke of this with you?" Blake asked, his brow furrowed.

"Yes. Not long before the whole incident here in the shop. He was such a good friend to me." Her voice cracked. "I thought I had finally found someone, anyone, who would understand. And then he was taken, arrested and…you know the rest."

"Oh, no," Merideth breathed, suddenly understanding why darkness hung over the girl next to her. Biting her lip, she inhaled deeply through her nose, hoping no one else noticed the panic welling within her.

TWELVE

Trappings of Craft

"WOULD anyone mind if I spoke to my sister alone?" Merideth asked sweetly. Pushing down her fear, she waited for their reply.

"Now?" Rider asked curtly. "She's my sister, too. And we just found out that she's good buddies with a murderer."

"He's a good man," Joseline defended hotly.

"You were saying about being calm?" Blake cut his eyes up at Sarah, who still held her tray.

"I think Hubert should go," Karen nearly shouted to be heard over the bickering, catching the others by surprise.

"And what's your say in all this?" Bert defended. "Aren't you just a clerk here?"

"I'm one of the people Morcant killed. I'd be dead if they hadn't resuscitated me." Karen's voice held an edge. "I'm a partner in this shop. I'm a full member of this coven. And I say you don't belong here."

"I call for a vote," Sarah added firmly, defending her best friend. "I vote he goes."

"I vote he goes as well," Merideth interjected, holding up her hand.

"Meri," Rider grunted. "We aren't part of these people," he hissed, leaning towards her.

"I don't care. I knew there was something off about them. Her, we have to help. She's family. Him? I'd rather see him away from us." Meri refused to budge.

Hearing her words, Joseline sighed. Standing, she muttered, "I believe I've made a mistake in coming here."

Catching her hand, Merideth pleaded, "Please don't leave."

Their digits firmly clenched, Jos pulled at the bond. Her skin burned where their flesh met. Glaring down at her younger sibling, she felt as if she stared into a mirror. "I vote that he goes."

The chaos ended abruptly, all eyes on her.

"You want me to leave?" Hubert huffed, getting to his feet.

"Yes. I'll call you. I promise." Her eyes fixed on Meri's, she had yet to look away.

"I bet," Bert snorted, slamming his mug onto the table. "Thanks for sticking up for me, Sis."

Sarah followed him to the door, locking it behind him. Pulling a thin string, she lowered the blinds that shielded the entrance from prying eyes, then scooted back to join the others. "Is she ok?" she asked, noting that no one else had moved, especially not the girl in question.

"I'm fine," Joseline croaked. "I just can't believe how much she looks like me." Dropping her sister's hand,

Meredith confessed, "I was thinking the same thing about you. It's hard to believe we have different fathers."

Reclaiming her chair, Joseline pulled at the chain around her neck, freeing her pendant. Fidgeting with the small flat stone, she sighed. "We do?" she asked absently. Her fingers toyed with her amulet, calming her raw nerves. "I guess you two share both parents?" she added, speaking to Rider.

"We don't share any parents," he stammered, opening his palms in doubt. "Meri is my girlfriend."

"Your girlfriend," Joseline echoed. "I thought we were siblings. The three of us." Her brow wrinkled with uncertainty.

"Well, we are, more or less." Meri grinned at the doubt on her sister's face. "Rider's father had him first, with a woman named Abigail."

"Dad says she died, but I have my suspicions," Rider explained gruffly.

"Then Thaddeus and my mother, Ezamay, had you," Meri continued, nodding as she spoke. "Then our mother married my father, Garrett, and they had me."

"I'm so confused," Joseline whined. Dropping her trinket, she pressed against her temples.

Noticing the gray colored amulet, Blake pursed his lips. "That's a very pretty necklace. Is it from the shop?" He glanced at the jewelry case his brother had installed years ago, hearing his brother's voice in his mind, calling it the 'trappings of the craft' at the time.

"Actually, Morc gave it to me." Her fingers flittered to caress it again, her lips parting into a small smile before it faded. "I didn't know what he did to you." She flicked her gaze between Karen and Sarah. "I'm sorry."

"Is she a seer as well?" Merideth asked hesitantly.

"She is gifted," Blake agreed. "But I don't think her skill is as pronounced as yours." Shifting, he moved to sit on the table before her, facing Joseline squarely. "You told Bert we were going to out you. What did you mean by that?"

"I…I'm a witch." She enunciated each word crisply. "Morcant told me so."

"And when was this," Blake prodded.

"One of the times he was placing an order. It was such a silly thing." She laughed at the memory. "See, there was this mouse," she began, then let the story fade. "I talk to animals," she finished flatly. "I have kept it hidden all my life. No one knew. No one else noticed, but he did." A large tear rolled down her cheek.

"Were you in love with Morcant?" Blake breathed, fear gripping his chest like a vice.

"Oh, no, not even." Joseline laughed, swiping away her drop of sadness. "We were the dearest of friends, that's all. He was never anything but kind, even generous, to me."

"Lucky you," Sarah bit angrily. She had more reason to hate Morcant than anyone, save maybe Karen. Watching her nimble fingers toy with the trinket, she mused, "He gave me a necklace once, too." It had been cursed, and nearly ended her.

Rising quickly, Blake pressed a stiff digit to his lips. "Shh. We don't want to frighten anyone, now do we?"

"Oh, no," Sarah whispered. "You don't think –"

"Shh," he repeated, cutting her off. "I don't know what I think, yet, and speculating isn't going to help."

Turning to the others, he clapped loudly. "Who's ready to return to the Korrigan mansion for a night of frivolity?"

"I'd rather have a good night's sleep," Rider growled.

"I should go home," Joseline declared, getting to her feet.

"But there's plenty of room," Merideth enticed. "We've been staying there as well. It would be nice, like a sleepover."

Joseline shook her head doubtfully. "But I thought we were going to see our mother. That's what you said." She glanced between their faces. "She's sick and that's why you came to find me."

The air grew heavy around them, no one speaking for a long moment. Clearing their dishes, Sarah sniffed.

"Why are you crying?" Rider asked, noticing the tears she hid behind a curtain of red hair.

"Oh, I don't know." She wiped at her cheeks. "We've all got mothers. I haven't seen mine in so long." The deluge fell, and she stopped trying to hide it. "Well, fuck." Leaving the tray of used cups, she went in search of a box of tissues.

"Yes," Meri agreed, snagging a few of the paper wipes and dabbing her eyes when she returned. "I'll take you to see our mother."

"Maybe tomorrow," Blake tacked on. "For tonight, come and stay with us. I'm sure the three of you have much to discuss."

"You're confident I won't be a burden?" Joseline asked, the temptation growing.

"Nope. Plenty of room," Blake confirmed. "Why don't you ride with these two, and they can swing by your place to pick up a bag. The girls and I will stop, grab dinner, and have that on to cook by the time you arrive."

"That sounds like a plan," Rider agreed, glancing at his watch. "We should get a move on."

"Then I guess it's settled," Meri chirped more cheerfully than she felt. Looping her arm through Joseline's, she beamed as she escorted her out to their car.

THIRTEEN

Magister's Trinket

INSIDE THE CAMARO, Sarah nearly exploded. "What the fuck was that, Blake?"

"What?" he asked innocently.

"You didn't tell her she has Morcant's death trinket hanging around her neck," Karen pointed out. "Do you think Merideth or Rider know?"

"Doubtful," Blake grunted. "We only know because of our past history with him. However, it is quite concerning."

"You think?" Sarah spat, still fuming. "I cannot believe this shit!" She held her long hair on both sides, pulling it firmly until her scalp tingled.

"Why would he give her a necklace like that, do you think?" Karen pondered. "He must have done it before he ever used the one against Sarah."

"It may have had a different purpose. She thinks they were good friends. Maybe he was manipulating her through it, somehow." Blake puckered his lips as he considered what his brother might have been up to.

"Maybe he still is," Sarah lamented.

"Are you going to at least tell them about the neck-lace?" Karen asked cautiously.

"I don't know yet," Blake clipped, pulling into the local market. "Let's get what we need so we can be at the house before they get there."

Across town, Joseline guided Rider onto her street. "That's it. The blue house on the left." She pointed at her pride and joy gleefully.

"That's a cute little place," Meri observed as they climbed out. "I haven't had much work this last year, but I'm an interior designer by trade," she added, itching to get her fingers on the place.

"Thanks." Joseline grinned. "I closed on it two weeks before the pandemic hit."

"Ouch." Rider winced. "At least my place is paid for."

"Hey, it's my place, too!" Meri clipped, punching his arm playfully.

"Well, yeah, but I bought it before we were together. Tomayto, tomahto…same thing." He swerved, goosing her with a gentle tickle, then pulling her into a firm hug. "You know this is going to be totally weird having a sister that looks like my girlfriend," he said quietly as Joseline let herself in.

"I know. Just make sure which one of us you're sleeping with," she teased.

"Ewww!" he moaned, following the other girl inside and hoping that would never be an issue. In another room, he could hear Joseline digging in a closet. "You need any help in there?"

"No. I'm getting a suitcase. I figure I should pack for

several days in case we decide to stay a while."

"She's taking this well," Merideth observed, sliding her arms around Rider's waist. "I'm not sure I could be this calm about it."

"What choice does she have?" he pointed out gently. "With your mother's illness, she doesn't have time to be upset." He bent over, kissing her forehead, then dropping lower to tease her lips. "I love you, Boo. I'm sorry I've been such a grouch."

"It's ok. We're all stressed right now." Raising her chin, she kissed him in return, deeper this time.

"Hey." Joseline coughed. "Do you mind? Seeing my brother kissing my sister will definitely take some getting used to."

"Not at all," Rider teased, planting a final smooch on his girl before releasing her. "I was actually just thinking the same thing, but we'll manage. I sure hope they have dinner ready when we get there, 'cause I'm starved." Picking up Joseline's bag for her, he headed to the car and dropped it in the trunk.

Behind the wheel once more, he used Google to find his way to Blake's place, and half an hour later they pulled up out front, parking behind the familiar Camaro.

"It's bigger than I remember," Jos observed.

"You've been here before?" Meri asked in surprise.

"Yeah. Morc brought me here. I think he was trying to keep me away from his coven, like I was a secret." She shivered. "It all seems so distorted. I used to think he cared a great deal about me. After meeting the girls and talking to Blake, I'm not so sure."

"You and Blake didn't really know each other?" Rider

asked, pulling her bag from the trunk. "I thought he was some big client of yours."

"M & J was my client." Joseline laughed. "Morcant ran the business, though. Before today, I've actually only spoken to Blake a couple of times, the big one being when he canned us."

"Wow. That must have stung," her sister commiserated.

"Not really. I wasn't happy, but it was before the economy shut down. At the time, I didn't realize how much it would cost us." The trio entered the living room, and Joseline giggled. "It's so odd being back here; and with you two, it's like everything is new."

"Come on," Merideth offered. "I'm sure they will let you have the room next to ours." Taking the stairs, she led the way, her siblings clomping noisily behind.

In the kitchen, Blake closed the oven, then paused to listen. "They're here."

"Yeah. They sound so happy," Karen observed.

"Why wouldn't they be?" Sarah shrugged. "They've found each other."

"And they have no idea about the necklace," Blake concluded.

"Should we tell them?" Sarah asked doubtfully.

"Not yet." Blake dropped his oven mitts on the counter. "Keep an eye on the steaks. I'm going to see how they're doing."

"I'll make the salad," Sarah volunteered.

"Great. Get it all ready, and I'll bring them down with me in a bit." Leaving the women to the preparations, Blake made hardly a sound as he crossed the front room. Heading down the stairs, a few creaked beneath his weight, but for the most part he remained stealthy.

Arriving at the room the trio occupied, he leaned on the door frame and grinned. "So, you three seem to be getting along."

Joseline cut her laugh off, pulling herself to attention. "We're fine, thank you, Blake. Is this room ok?"

"This room is sufficient." He smirked at her formality. "You are a welcome guest, Josee."

"Josee," she snapped. "Oh, no no no. My name is Joseline. 'Jaws-ee' as in egg-and lynn. No ee's. Jos if you need to make short, but it's pronounced 'jaws'."

He only laughed, wafting a hand at them. "Dinner is in the oven. Come down and join us."

"Ugh, it's been such a long day," Meri chirped, her fingers encircling her sister's arm. "Do you enjoy wine? We should have stopped for some."

"The girls picked some up. You and Josee are welcome to a glass or two." Blake beamed, waiting for the reaction.

"It's not Josee!" She closed the distance, smacking his arm with an open palm.

"Come on. It's never too late to try something new." His grin faded as the amulet around her neck caught his eye.

Noting his fixation, her fingers caressed the stone. "Does it bother you that Morc gave it to me?"

"No." He hesitated, flicking his gaze at Rider and Merideth. "Let's talk about that later, shall we?" He stepped back, indicating the portal with an open palm.

Joseline led the way down the stairs and to the kitchen. "Oh, this is quite a spread," she observed. The table was small, and the six chairs around it left little elbow room. The center held a selection of sides and a salad, with a plate piled with steaks atop a lazy-Susan. "What if I'm a vegetarian?"

"Then, you get to eat the sides." Karen giggled, admiring Joseline's spunk.

"Josee," Blake emphasized her new nickname, "is pulling your leg. She is perfectly happy with a hearty steak."

"And how would you know that?" she demanded, still miffed at him.

"Just a hunch. Seriously, if you need something else, we have some canned goods. You could have some spinach. Maybe a little corn."

"Very funny." She scowled to hide her laugh, trying not to like him as much as she did. "Don't think I don't know you, Blake Korrigan. I've seen you around." Taking her seat, she glared at him.

"Do tell," Merideth urged. "I'd love to hear more about our host, especially from a sister's perspective."

"Oh, he's quite the womanizer from what I hear," Jos cooed. "That fast car of his isn't the only thing that runs…hot."

"Hey now." Blake's lips drew into a thin line. "Sarah and I have been together well over a year. Nearly two."

"Which only leads me to wonder how she keeps you in line?" The words dripped sweetly, the venom hidden inside.

"And here I thought we were all getting along so nicely." Karen stabbed a steak and hoisted it to her plate.

"Just setting the ground rules, love," Blake growled,

his authority clear. "I love my Sarah very deeply. I have no need to prowl around."

"Please don't spoil the evening," Sarah begged quietly. Cutting her eyes over at Joseline, she caught a glint of light off the stone hanging beneath her chin. Catching her breath, she gasped. "Oh, Josee. Your pendant."

"Dammit, Blake. Now everyone is going to call me that!" Jos slapped her leg with loud disgust.

"It's ok." He chuckled, amused at her displeasure. Taking a few gulps of his wine, he returned the glass gently to the table. "I guess we can't ignore it, can we."

"Ignore what?" She continued her tirade, her face flushed.

"Can you remove the amulet?" Blake asked calmly. "Or do you always wear it?"

"The amulet?" Her chest heaved. "Why are you so obsessed with your brother's gift to me?"

"Morcant gave me a necklace once, too." Sarah spoke up, her fingers fiddling with her fork. "He used it to transform me into Brenna. He cursed me with it, controlling me. Bending me to his will."

"That's preposterous," Joseline bellowed, her eyes darting from face to face.

"You do seem a bit angry," Rider pointed out. "A few minutes ago, we were laughing and enjoying each other's company."

Seated next to her, Meri strained to see the stone. "I didn't realize cursing objects was so popular."

"You've seen it done before?" Joseline's voice lost a bit of anger when she addressed her almost-twin.

"A feather. My mother put a spell on it, or on me,

through it." She blinked at the other woman a few times. "Our mother. Sorry."

"Our mother casts curses," Jos whispered.

"Oh, no. It wasn't really a curse," Rider interceded, seeing where this was going. "Ezamay is a fine woman."

Breathing slowly, Joseline's fingers toyed with the magister's trinket. "I take it off when I shower. And when I sleep," she offered. "I have a place where I lay it so that I can still see it, though."

"Have you ever tried to leave it. Or not wear it?" Blake probed.

Joseline swallowed. "I can't," she alleged. "I always thought it was because Morc was so dear to me." Her brown eyes flicked up, staring into the calmness of the ice blue across from her. "You look so much like him, Blake, and yet you are so different."

"Did you sleep with him?" their host pushed.

She blinked rapidly, a single tear escaping to run down her check. "Yes. Well, I think I did."

"He inducted her," Karen observed in a hushed tone.

"Yes, he pulled her in," Blake quietly agreed. "I'm sorry, Joseline. My brother has treated you with the same cold calculation as he has most others in his life."

"But what about the necklace?" Rider interrupted. "If that is the source of her strange behavior, can't we just get rid of it?"

"If only it were that simple." Sarah sighed, dabbing her lips with a napkin. Looking around the table, she lamented, "We have this beautiful meal, yet none of us can enjoy it."

"Not while one of us is hurting," Karen agreed.

FOURTEEN

One Old Crone

DINNER CONTINUED IN A SOMBER FASHION, each of them slaking their hunger while their souls yearned. The tightness of their group unconfirmed, they each felt a connection to those around them—a dark connection—with Morcant Korrigan at its center.

"Do you think he could have planned this?" Sarah asked absently.

"I don't see how," Rider obliged, waving his fork for emphasis.

Swallowing his bite hurriedly, Blake gulped more wine. Placing the empty glass on the table, he stewed. "My brother is a bastard. There's no telling what he planned. Or what he didn't. He uses all things to his advantage when he has the means." He eyed Joseline warily, noting she had hidden the trinket inside her blouse.

"You removed the amulet from Sarah," Josee mused aloud. "Maybe you could do the same for me."

"Ah, but we had a lot of help at the time. We won't be

able to do that again." He glanced between Sarah and Karen. "Unless one of you happens to have an old crone lying around."

Karen snorted, laughing at the inside joke. Joining her, the whole group caught the giggles for a moment before the wave of joviality subsided.

"Seriously." Merideth mellowed. "How did you defeat him last time?"

Elbows on the table, Blake folded his hands at his chin to lean on. "Come now, dear. I don't believe that's a story you really want to hear." He cut his eyes over at her newly found sister in warning.

"I, for one, would like to hear it," Joseline countered, sitting up straighter in her chair. "Do tell."

"Yes, I think we should all be interested in how you defeated the dark and powerful Morcant," Rider teased.

Squinting at him, Blake's lower lip pooched out.

Raising his hands, Rider appeased, "Hey, I'm just saying. If we're going to figure this out, we're going to need all the information we can get. Please, share." He extended a palm towards his new friend.

"The question is, where to begin," Karen lamented.

"No, the real question is, do we have enough wine?" Blake raised his empty glass for emphasis.

Rising, Sarah went to pull a few bottles from her secret stash. "There is always wine, Babe. I don't think I could function without it." Opening the bottle, she topped the glasses, starting with her lover's. "I'll start. Karen took me to a bizarre where she helped Morcant give me the amulet. He had cursed it and used it later that night to gain access to my room."

Sitting back in her chair gruffly, she held her glass

high to prevent from spilling it. Steady in her seat, she lowered it slowly, watching it come down. When it reached her lap, she sighed. "He raped me through a dream. That's how it started."

"Oh, Sarah," Meri breathed. "I'm so sorry. Maybe this is one story we don't need to hear."

"What about me? Like she said, I helped him." Karen took a swig. "Not that I had any real choice. He does that to you. Makes your mind all foggy."

"And you have no control," Joseline finished for her.

"Is that how you ended up in bed with him?" Rider asked, swirling his glass.

"In bed." Jos coughed a short laugh. "It wasn't anything so romantic as that. It was more like on the couch, in there." She pointed to the living room. "We were sitting together on it. One minute, I was telling him I wasn't interested in men. And the next I was under him, naked." She shivered. "I had totally blacked it out until tonight."

"All right. I'll tell the rest of it," Blake stated firmly, glancing around at the group. Diving in, he picked the story up from Sarah's unfortunate encounter and drove straight through. His telling as antiseptic as possible, he tried to keep the tears to a minimum, as each part of the story held pain, and often regret, for someone.

When he had finished, he stood, placing his glass in the sink. "And with that, ladies and gentleman, I'm going to bed."

"Yeah, me too," Sarah agreed. "I'll come down and do the dishes in the morning before I make breakfast." She stood, following him out.

The remaining four watched them go, a little surprised at their hasty departure.

"I thought we'd at least get the chance to talk about it," Rider grumbled.

"Let it digest," Karen suggested. "I lived it, and almost two years later, I still don't really understand all of it."

"Should we follow suit, or clean up before we retire?" Meri asked, doubtful about leaving such a filthy mess until morning.

"You two go on. Have a little private time. Karen and I can take care of this," Joseline offered, giving the other girl a wink.

"Are you sure? I mean, you're a guest!" Merideth's brow furrowed.

"So are you." Karen giggled, hearing the ceiling above them creak. "Go on. I know you could probably use some alone time."

"Don't argue, Boo." Rider got to his feet, using her arm to help her up as well. The chandelier above the table swayed slightly. "We need to get out of this room before those two bring the roof down on us."

As soon as they were gone, Karen burst into peals of laughter. Helping herself to the remainder of the bottle, she sighed. "I wondered if he would notice."

"Is that Blake and Sarah's room above us?" Jos stared at the swaying lamp.

"Yeah. But don't worry, they do this every night." Karen took a noisy sip. "It hasn't come down yet."

"Great to know." Joseline clapped her hands against her thighs, getting to her feet. "Know any spells for grease?"

"Yeah, dish soap," Karen teased, joining her at the sink.

Together, they scraped and scrubbed, clearing the table and loading the dishwasher. The conversation flowed between them easily, making the chore less of a burden.

"Does your leg hurt much?" Joseline asked at one point, indicating Karen's cane. "I can finish if you need to sit for a while."

"No, it doesn't hurt." Karen glanced at the door, then stole a cigarette out of Blake's box of reds. "You don't mind if I have one, do you?"

"I didn't know you smoked. Or is it because of me?"

"You? What would you have to do with it?" Karen lit the end, then sat after all.

"I make people nervous. I always have," Joseline confessed. "No matter where I was, I never quite fit."

"I think you fit here," Karen observed.

"Yes, but here isn't a real place, is it." Jos raised her eyebrows with her question, then continued to load the machine. "Meri and Rider will go home soon."

"Will you follow them?" Karen flicked her ashes into one of the plates.

"Don't do that." Joseline gagged. "It's disgusting."

"Sorry," Karen mumbled. Standing, she hobbled to the living room to retrieve an ashtray. When she returned, she observed, "Maybe Meri will stay here. We all agree she would make a great addition to the coven."

"But not Rider," Joseline added.

"Oh, no. He would be welcome, but he keeps insisting he's non-practicing. Kind of defeats the purpose of joining a coven." Karen giggled. "I do like him, though. His grouchy ass is funny."

"I know." Jos smiled as well. "And Merideth adores him, which is why she won't stay without him. No, if he returns to NOLA, she'll go."

Karen's grin faded. "You know that Meri is a seer."

"Yes. She has already discovered a few things out about me I thought I had well hidden." Closing the washer, she set the dial. "That's all we can do for now. The rest will have to wait, as Sarah predicted."

"I think you see things as well," Karen dared.

"No, not nearly as well as my sister," Joseline denied, reaching for Karen's cane and offering it to her.

Her smoke gone, Karen accepted the stick, staring up at her new friend. "But you do *see*."

"I see you." Joseline nodded. "Have you told anyone?"

"No." Karen shook her dark locks. "I've been waiting, I guess. I'm moving back to Atlanta after graduation. I figure I'll tell my parents first. I think coming out to them before anyone else would be fitting."

Deciding she wasn't ready to leave the coziness of the kitchen, Joseline took one of the empty chairs. "The swaying stopped," she pointed out casually, indicating the light above them.

"Maybe." Karen giggled. "It could just be a recess."

"Oh." Joseline grinned. "Does Sarah know? About you?"

"Sarah…" Karen's voice trailed away, and she rubbed her chin thoughtfully. "Sarah is probably the reason why."

"Oh, rubbish. If that's what you think, you aren't

ready to come out. You're still not sure. You don't really understand," Joseline accused.

"I understand perfectly," Karen clipped. "While my best friend was busy fucking strange men, she and I hooked up."

"You and Sarah were together." Joseline bounced her finger back and forth, making the connection. "Do you regret it?"

"No. Hell no." Karen reached for Blake's pack. Pausing before lighting the tip, she added thoughtfully, "I regret that I didn't enjoy it." She applied the flame and took a long drag. "I wish we could do it again, and I'd take my time. I'd make sure she knew how much I loved her."

"Nice. Maybe you are ready." Joseline reached for the box, fishing out one for herself. "These are disgusting. You should try the flavored ones."

"Maybe we will some time." Karen grinned at her. "Let's go upstairs. I'll show you some pictures of Sarah before she got all Brennafied."

"You don't have any on your phone?" Joseline asked, taking a short drag and puffing bits of smoke.

"Nope. She deleted them all. I'm sure her parents still have some, but any device she could get her hands on, she purged."

"Wow. She must have been bitter. I don't sense that from her now."

"Oh my God!" Karen sat up straight. "I knew it!"

"Calm down. I told you, I'm not a seer."

"But you read people. Like, their emotions and stuff," Karen stated gleefully. "Do you really talk to animals or were you just making that up?"

"No, I do communicate with them. I think it's connected to the emotions, though. Like I'm just reading them as well. Empathic, I think it would be called." She glanced at her cigarette, which had neared the end. "Let's go up, and you can show me those pics. I'd love to see who Sarah was before she found herself."

"Found herself," Karen scoffed. "I doubt she would see it that way."

"Yeah, but that doesn't make it any less true."

Karen stood, using her cane to shuffle to the door. "My old leg is stiff tonight," she mumbled, fighting her way up the stairs.

"Take your time." Joseline followed, doing her best not to rush her. At the top, she noticed the hall branched after the room shared by Rider and Meri, hers being the first one they had come to. Glancing down the hall to the right, she pointed, "Is that the end over the kitchen?"

"Yeah. That's Sarah and Blake down there." A sharp thud echoed from the darkened hallway, and Karen giggled. "Sorry. They go all night sometimes."

"Well, I guess we see how she keeps him in line," Joseline mused.

"Yeah, I guess that's it. My room is this way." A little further down, the main hall made a sharp left, with more bedrooms on either side. At the end, a closed door hid the place Karen called home.

"Damn this place is huge." Joseline looked back, counting to herself. "Ten bedrooms?"

"There's a few more downstairs. I think they are servant's quarters, though. I like mine because it has a private bath. Some of the others have to share." She opened her portal. "Don't mind the mess."

Glancing around at her laundry strewn floor, Joseline laughed. "You must not get much company up here."

"Nope. I avoid people. Not hard, with the pandemic." Reaching into her closet, she stretched, feeling along the top shelf. "Damn it."

"Here. Let me get that," Joseline offered. Her reach a little better, she pulled the floral print box down with one try. "Here you go." She stood toe to toe with her host, holding out her offering.

"Thanks." Karen accepted it. Her brown eyes met those before her. "You don't really look like her, you know."

"Like who? Meri?"

"Yeah. I mean you guys favor, you can tell you're related, but you don't really look like her. Your eyes have these golden flecks in them. And your face is shaped different," Karen explained, her cheeks flushed.

"Thanks." Jos swallowed. Holding up her hand, she indicated the bed. "Shall we?"

"Oh." Karen's pink flush turned bright red. "Oh, you mean the pictures!" She laughed anxiously, hobbling over to sit on the edge of her mattress. Turning, she dumped the box, the memories spilling out.

Sitting on the mattress with her, Joseline gave her some room. "Aww, you guys were so cute!" She fished out a few, holding them up in the dim light. "You never see real pictures anymore."

"I know." Karen searched through the pile. "Here's a good one. This is from high school."

Taking the photo, Joseline sighed. "She really isn't bitter anymore, Karen. She's…comfortable with her new self."

"I know. I just feel guilty. If I hadn't helped him," Karen began, her voice not letting her finish the thought.

"If you hadn't helped him, he would have found another way," Joseline stated firmly. She could feel her new friend's guilt radiating from her. "It wasn't your fault." Catching her chin, her slender fingers lifted Karen's face. Looking her in the eye, she used a thumb to caress her cheek. "You are going to make some woman very lucky, some day."

"But it won't be Sarah," Karen tacked on, pulling away as a tear escaped. Swiping at it, she cursed. "Damn it."

"Sarah loves you," Josee observed. "Just not that way, hon."

"Tell me something I don't know," Karen spat. Scooping the pictures into their box, she ground her teeth. "I've known her my whole life. She was mine first!"

"Aww, Karen." Joseline took the box from her, placing on the desk beside the bed. Sitting back on the mattress, their legs rubbed. Normally, it would mean she was too close, but not tonight. "Let's make love," she offered boldly.

"What?" Karen's face shot up and she glared at her. "Casual? Just like that?"

Joseline leaned forward to kiss her, pausing a breath away from Karen's lips. "I won't force you. But I'm here. I'd love to lay with you."

Karen panted, her hand on the other woman's chest as she held her at bay. When Joseline stayed put, it left her no choice. She could either accept the invitation or be the one to move away.

FIFTEEN

Secret Garden

BENEATH HER PALM, Karen could feel Joseline's heart beating her breast. Relaxing, her hand cupped the mound and sighed. Raising her chin, she closed the gap, pressing their lips together. Parting them, she opened herself, then whispered, "I love this. You feel so soft, Josee."

Pushing her back, onto her pillow, Joseline held herself above her with a stiff arm. "Are you sure? We had a lot of wine tonight."

"This isn't the wine," Karen insisted. Her hand shot up, using her fingers to explore her supple neck, then ear, and finally wavey brown hair. "I wasted it last time. I won't make that mistake again."

Closing her eyes, Joseline pressed against her, full force. Her lips trailing her throat, she toyed with her. Then standing, she hauled the other girl to her feet using one of her arms.

"What are you doing?" Karen gasped, afraid she had changed her mind.

"Uh." Joseline couldn't think. Her mind had become

trapped, focused on one thing. Reaching for her, she kissed Karen again, slowly. Urgently. "I have nothing with me. It's just me in this room."

"That's all I need," Karen assured. Pushing past her, she closed the door and locked it. A silly thing, really. Any butter knife could open it, but it gave the illusion of privacy.

Pivoting slowly, she faced the other girl. "How do we do this?" She panted. "Do we take it slow and undress each other, or just tear off our close and go at it." Her features brightened. "I almost forgot!" Pulling out a drawer, she held it out.

"Oh, my!" Joseline gasped. "Your collection is huge."

"Yeah. I've been ordering them from different places. Trying them out."

"Do you know what this one's for?" Joseline asked, fishing out a slender silver one.

"Yeah." Karen grinned eagerly. "Let me use them on you."

"Use them on me?" Joseline raised her brows.

"Yes. I've been practicing. Let me show you." She dropped the drawer, yanking her shirt over her head. Pulling at the button on her pants, she had them off as well before she stopped, noting Joseline hadn't moved.

"What's the matter?" Had she changed her mind?

Her breathing erratic, Josee stared at her. "I'm scared."

Karen blinked rapidly. "You're scared. Why would you be scared? You've done this like a million times, right?"

Joseline's jaw dropped, then she clamped it shut. "Not like a million," she defended. "I've been with a few girls.

I love girls." She breathed, grinning sheepishly. Getting ahold of herself, she smoothed her blouse. "This could be serious, though."

"But you offered," Karen whined loudly. "I thought you wanted this!"

"I do." Joseline stepped towards her. "Trust me, baby, I do. I know this sounds crazy, but I don't want to mess it up."

Karen blinked at her. "You're not thinking of a one-night stand."

"No." Joseline shook her head. "I've had my share, and that's not how this feels. I'm afraid if we do this, one of us will get hurt."

"Oh." Karen wrapped herself in her arms, thinking it over. Lifting her chin, she announced, "I'm willing to risk it. Let me use my toys on you." She indicated her collection.

"Oh, Karen." Joseline laughed. Her eyes bright, she held the grin. "Our secret, then? I won't out you, I promise." Her fingers nimble, she unbuttoned her blouse and it floated to the floor. Opening Morcant's chain, she placed it on the desk for safe keeping.

Karen watched as Josee removed the rest, each item a small tease at what lay underneath. When she removed her panties, Karen gasped. "You're clean shaven!"

"Waxed," Joseline corrected. She knew it wouldn't be tender. All new to Karen, it wouldn't be sexy lovemaking. Taking the other girl's hand, she used it to massage her vulva. "I like to keep it tidy. I think of it as my secret garden."

"Wow, that's smooth." Karen flushed, imagining her

own fur. She trimmed it, but it certainly wasn't waxed. "My garden is a mess."

"Show me yours," Joseline suggested. "It can't be that bad."

Dropping her bra first, Karen stalled. But with nothing else to remove, it was time to put up or shut up. Pulling at her panties, she slid them down her legs. At least those were shaven. Dropping them around her ankles, she straightened, waiting for the verdict.

When their eyes met, Joseline still smiled. "Can I touch you now?"

"Oh my God, you don't have to ask! Yes, touch me. Please!" Karen felt a rush of relief. Fear and excitement twisted her gut. When Joseline reached her, their mouths met, each hungrily searching, exploring the other.

Their hands roamed freely over their bare flesh for several minutes before Karen's leg grew tired. "You need to lay down?" Joseline prodded.

"That or sit," Karen confessed. "You lay down. Let me explore." Picking up her box of toys, she waited for Josee to comply.

Stretching, Joseline slunk onto the covers, turning to lay face up. Her perky breasts formed pink points on her chest. Karen happily ran her fingers eagerly over the flesh, wrinkling them. Then she bent over, pulling the left into her mouth. Joseline jumped, not quite trusting what she would do with it, but Karen worked it gently. Her tongue teasing the tight nipple, she ended the sucking motion before pulling away. "It feels good. I like the way it tickles my tongue."

Joseline relaxed, letting her lover explore. When Karen slid down, she moved her leg, granting her access the goods hidden between them. "Oh my God, your clit is pierced!" Karen flicked it with her finger, then used her tongue. "Oh, that feels so weird. And it's warm."

Joseline exhaled slowly, her arm resting across her forehead. "Maybe I should go first. And then you can do me."

"Not a chance." Karen reached into her pleasure bucket to select an instrument. Deciding on a simple version, her mind dove to Sarah's memory, the night she had used her only model on her. Shoving the thought aside, she applied the jellied phallus, rubbing against the labia and around the pussy before her. "You aren't very wet," she observed.

"I'm nervous. Do you have any lube?"

Karen paused, considering. "You're not enjoying this." She sat up. "We should stop."

Joseline sighed, sitting up to face her. "If we stop, then it just becomes awkward."

"As if this isn't." Karen stared at her toy. "I wanted to show you I was good at this." She paused, rolling her tongue. "I wanted to *be* good at this."

Joseline leaned forward. Her hand on Karen's shoulder, she squeezed. Their lips brushing, she sighed. "Then stop trying so hard. Is this really what you wanted to do to Sarah?"

Karen winced at the other girl's name, looking away. "No."

"Then show me. What did want to give her?"

Karen sighed. "Can we turn off the light?"

"Sure." Joseline removed the fake dick from her grasp and dropped it in the box, placing it on the floor. Standing, she cut off the light, then waited to let her eyes adjust. "Oh, this is dark."

A hand grasped her hip. "Yeah. I like it dark."

"It doesn't scare you?" Joseline whispered.

"No." Karen inched her way around. Behind her, she forgot all about her leg. Pressing the full front of her nakedness against her, she teased her nipples with Joseline's back. Rough, then smooth, she felt of her new front. At the belly button, she flattened her right palm, continuing down until she met the smooth pubic bone and the bulge of flesh.

Working her, Karen breathed against her neck. The same height, they matched perfectly. Her fingers searching, she massaged her clit, then pushed back the hood. Beneath it, the metal teased her fingers as she used her left arm to hug Joseline firmly, then massaged her breasts. Squeezing, pinching, then rubbing while she panted against her neck.

Releasing her, she pushed her forward to the bed. "Back or front?"

Her words sharp, Joseline hesitated.

"Fine. Front." Karen shoved her onto the bed. Landing haphazardly, Joseline adjusted, pulling her knees up beneath her. Her breaths short, she panted into the blanket as Karen knelt behind her, using her tongue to explore every crevice.

Relaxing, Jos pushed against the fingers that slipped inside her. Moaning, she encouraged the thrusts, pouting when they were removed. A moment later, a slick dildo took their place. "Oh God."

Gentle, then rough, Karen toyed with her. Her tongue tired easily, but her fingers knew what to do. "Roll over," she urged, pushing on a hip and removing the dick from Josee's wetness.

On her back, Joseline peered into the darkness, able to make out the ceiling above them. Her body on fire, she groaned. Karen showed her no mercy, pushing her over the edge into an explosive orgasm. Jos trembled, whimpering slightly as her back arched against the bedding.

Kissing the inside of her thighs, Karen removed the toy, dropping it on the floor. Slithering up her slender frame, she lay over the older woman. "That's what I would do to her," she whispered.

SIXTEEN

On the Clock

RISING THE NEXT MORNING, a smile lingered on Merideth's lips. She and Rider had made love the night before, and for the first time in months, it had felt good to be with him. As if his tenderness suited her and she didn't need the pain.

Dressed in a casual suit, she pulled up her hair. Still messing with her bun as she left the room, she paused at the next door. Standing open, Joseline's chamber remained immaculate. Stepping over the threshold, she glanced around, noting her sister's suitcase was missing. Her lips puckered, she contemplated where she might have gone. "Surely she didn't run away," she muttered, taking the stairs.

Making it to the kitchen, Meri found someone to interrogate. Standing at the sink, Sarah finished off the dishes left from the night before. "Where is she?" Meri gasped for air, terrified of the answer.

"Who?" Sarah asked, not looking up from her chore.

"Josee! Her bag isn't in her room."

"Maybe she changed rooms," Rider suggested, coming in behind her. "This house has a dozen of them."

Seated at the table and scrolling on a tablet, a bare-chested Blake waved a hand. "She isn't gone, if that's what you're worried about."

"How do you know?" Meri clipped, wringing her hands as she took one of the empty chairs and focused on not looking at his hair-covered chest. "And why aren't you dressed?"

"I haven't had my breakfast yet. Then I shower, then I dress." Blake shook his head, as if she should have known that.

"Good morning everyone," Karen sang, sauntering into the kitchen with Joseline hot on her heels.

Blake simply pointed, grinning at the girl across from him.

Pouring coffee, Rider also took a seat. "Good morning. I guess we should eat up and get on the road."

Meri gaped at him. "I guess we can." Her eyes flittered between the two women who had just arrived. Her mind raced, at least until she realized she might be the only one picking up on the vibe. "I need some coffee."

"Here you go." Sarah placed a mug before her. "Anyone else while I'm pouring?"

Karen and Joseline exchanged a glance, then Karen slipped into an empty seat. "I'll take some."

Taking the vacant next to her, Josee agreed, "Sounds good. Do we get breakfast, as well?"

"Shortly." Sarah beamed, as if she were earning a tip. "Eggs and sausage are on the way."

"Well, everyone sure seems chipper considering where we left off last night," Rider observed. Helping himself to a slice of toast already on the table, he waved it around at the group. "Are we all going, or is it just the three of us?"

Placing more plates on the table, Sarah paused, noticing the way her best friend and Joseline leaned into each other. "Thank you, ladies, for taking care of the dishes." The duo ignored her, their eyes locked as they whispered to each other.

"They seem a little preoccupied," Blake observed calmly, also helping himself to the toast.

Leaning forward, Karen planted a huge kiss on Joseline's lips. Parting them, their intensity left no doubts, and she didn't care who saw.

"I did *not* see that coming," Rider dropped flatly.

"Don't judge," Blake commanded, noticing Meri's grimace. "What? As a seer, did you think you would know everything ahead of time?"

"No." She laughed at him, the giggle not reaching her eyes.

"Well good, because you won't. Ever." His gaze flicked to Sarah, who had returned to the stove. "I think we all need to go."

"Why would we all go?" Sarah asked, keeping her back to the table and hoping the groping would be over before she served the rest of the plates.

Joseline ended the kiss, her hand caressing her lover's face. "I would love for all to come. But why are we driving? Wouldn't it be faster to fly?"

"Oh, no. I hate flying," Merideth informed them sharply.

"Are you saying you drove here? From New Orleans?" She gasped, calculating the distance.

"No, we flew from NOLA," Rider explained. "We rented the car in Virginia and have driven since then."

"You drove from Virginia to Boston?" Sarah placed the last plates on the table. "Sorry, but I don't fancy being cramped in a car for two days to go see someone else's mother." Her eyes finally meeting Karen's, she glared at her.

"We don't all have to go. Really, only the three of us need to make the trip," Rider pointed out, taking a plate of food.

"Or the two of us." Meri snorted.

"The two of you?" Her mate paused, staring at her. "You want to leave me here with these guys while you and Josee go see your mother?"

"She is my mother," Meri clipped, also giving Karen a sideways glance.

"Are you all mad because they slept together?" Blake demanded. "Because that's what it looks like." He used a flat palm to indicate the new couple as he spoke. "Ezamay is my friend and I certainly have a right to visit her."

"Pfft, please." Merideth raised her chin. "You haven't thought of her in years. And not that I'm judging, but Josee is my sister. To have some chick hook up with her at a time like this—"

"It was my idea," Joseline cut her off. Standing, she rested her hand on Karen's shoulder, giving it a squeeze. "Who I hook up with is my business. I am the older sister here."

"And I'm the big brother," Rider snapped, wiping his face with a napkin before tossing it across his plate. Also standing, his blue orbs darted between them. "Your idea, huh? Don't you know to keep that shit to the outside? When you two go south, and it will, it poisons the relationship for everyone else."

"What do you care? You're going back to NOLA anyway," Karen pointed out sharply.

"That's not the point!" Rider shouted.

"The point is, that thing around her neck hasn't lost any of its charm." Blake stood, glaring at the rest of them. "Have you people not learned anything?"

"What are you saying?" Merideth asked more calmly. "You think the amulet is causing us to fight?"

"It's a strong possibility. We won't know until we get it off of her. Now, can everyone just shut up and eat? We'll figure out who all is going and how we are getting there, afterwards." Blake had spoken and the fight stopped there. Retaking his seat, he scooped an egg onto his plate.

Reluctantly, the rest followed suit. Dirty looks were passed between bites, but no one spoke until the last plate had been placed in the sink.

Inhaling, then releasing the breath slowly, Sarah asked, "Shall I load the dishwasher?"

"That's fine." Blake stood, agreeing to the task. "The rest of us will go in the living room; you can join us when you're done."

"So, now I'm the maid," she bit tartly. On her feet, she started water and located a brush.

"You're not the maid, Babe." He bent to kiss her nose on the way by. "I know you. I'll be sure you are represented." Patting her on the rear, he sauntered out. Flopping onto the near end of the sofa, he picked up his pack

SAMANTHA JACOBEY

of cigarettes. Fishing one out, he lit it, waiting for the others to join him.

Merideth took a seat in the chair on the far side of the room while Rider took her end of the couch, which formed a corner with the table between them, leaving a full cushion length between him and their host. "I think we should get that thing off her neck before we take her to see Ezamay," he stated without preamble.

"But we're on the clock," Meri groused. "We don't even know how to get it off. We can't afford to wait."

Settling into the chair facing her sister, Joseline winced. "I have to agree. It's been harmless all these years, so surely I can visit one dying mother with it on."

Taking the cushioned arm next to her, Karen sighed. "I would like to go as well, but not if it makes a fuss. I can wait here."

"Nonsense." Joseline took her hand, folding it into hers. "Neither shop is doing enough business to lose sleep over. Let's all pack up and go to Virginia. The question is, do we drive or fly."

"We fly," Blake stated bluntly. "Driving would be too painful under the given circumstances. However, we can't just leave at the drop of a hat. We need to have someone in charge of the store."

"We've only been open a few days," Karen pointed out. "I doubt anyone will miss us."

"That's not the point. It's still a sensitive place. We have things in there that should be looked after. We can't just leave town with no one to keep an eye on it." Blake took a long drag, pondering their predicament. "I have someone. I'll go arrange it this afternoon. You all get us booked on a flight, and we'll need a van to fit all

134

of us once we get there." Standing, he turned to the stairs, ready to go up and have his shower, then get dressed.

"How do you like that?" Rider clicked his tongue. "He acts like he's in charge."

"He's the magister," Sarah informed him, joining them from the kitchen. "He is in charge."

"We aren't part of your coven," Rider retorted.

Sarah only laughed, marching over to the stairs. "Make the reservations and don't piss him off."

"Madam Demore?" Blake called into the small room. Dimmer than usual, only a handful of candles had been lit.

The beaded curtain on the back wall shook. "Judoc! I had no idea you would come for a visit." She shuffled in, presenting him with a brief hug. "I wasn't feeling well this morning, so I left the lights low," she explained, indicating the walls.

"I see. But I haven't come for a reading," he clarified. "I need to leave town for a few days. I was wondering if you might spend a few hours at the shop for us. Just go in and have a look around. Make sure no one's broken in or anything like that."

"Afraid of losing your treasures." She laughed at her own joke. "Or more concerned about what your brother is up to."

Blake's jaw dropped. "And here I didn't think I was here for a reading. You think Morcant is up to something?"

"Hard to say." She shrugged. "You Korrigans were always up to something back in the day."

"What about now," he persisted. "I mean, what can he do from prison, right?"

She stared at him, not bothering to respond.

"Shit. I was afraid of that." He ran his fingers roughly around his lips. "Ok, will you go by and visit the shop? You don't have to hang out there. Just go in, have a look around, then lock up when you go."

"How long will you be gone?"

"Maybe a week. I'm not really sure. You don't have to go every day. Every other day, maybe."

"This I will do for you," she assured. "Do I get a key?"

"Yeah." He pulled the ring from his pocket, sliding the key around the loop a few times to free it. "Here you go." Holding it out to her, he waited.

"You are afraid," she observed, taking the shiny bit of medal.

"Not for me," he replied sharply. "I've done a lot of living. I'm ok if anything happens to me."

"But…"

"But, I have a house full of kids now. They're all so young. Totally wet behind the ears, you know?"

"As you once were," she suggested calmly.

"Yeah. And now, it's all on me. If I fuck this up, they're the ones who're going to suffer."

"That choice is not up to you," she reminded him gently. "You make your decision and then you live with it. Let the chips fall where they may."

"Yeah. I was afraid you'd say that." He turned, ready to leave. "Thanks for looking after the place. You have my number if you need to reach me?" he asked at the door.

"I have your number, yes, but all will be fine. Have faith, Judoc. You will make a good magister to your coven."

"Thanks. I hope so," said more to himself as he pulled the door wide to exit.

SEVENTEEN

Old Tricks

THE GROUP ARRIVED at the airport in plenty of time to check in and make it through security. Making the reservations had fallen to Merideth since she was the pickiest of the lot, and she had secured a minivan for the trip to her parents' home. She and Rider stopped to turn in their current rental while the rest of the group moved through, but they caught up at their gate where they waited to board.

Walking up to the people he had somehow come to think of as friends, Rider grinned. "Are you guys having an argument without me?"

"No, just a discussion," Josee quipped, tossing her long brown hair. "Too bad you are non-practicing, or we could talk about yours."

"My what?" Rider bit, placing his carryon next to a post and closing the circle with his tall frame.

"Your talent. It seems that we all have one," she continued, glaring at their red-head. "Sarah here is a caster. She knows hundreds of spells, don't you, June bug?"

Sarah scowled at her. "I know a few. I told you. I love to learn them, to collect them, like butterflies or something."

"But you also use them," Joseline added emphatically.

"Lots of people cast," Blake interrupted, glancing around. "I'm not sure this is a discussion for such a crowded place. New subject, please."

"Well, we could talk about the cat." Joseline crossed her arms. "I got to pet her before we left the house. It was very enlightening." Her eyes bore into Sarah, who turned ghost white.

"Oh, isn't she beautiful?" Merideth sang. "Her name is Caly. Such a sweet kitten."

"Actually, she's a real witch," Jos dropped flatly.

Meri's head snapped to glare at her sister. "Why the hell would you say that?"

Blake stepped into the middle of their ring. "Because she can't follow orders, that's why. I said this was a discussion for another time."

"Oh, come on. No one cares what we're talking about," Joseline informed him tartly. Leaning closer to her near twin, she said more quietly, "Because Sarah cursed her. She's a human."

Meri gasped, staring at the girl in question. "Is that true?" Sarah only fidgeted.

"She had it coming," Karen defended. "She was helping Morcant, who tried to kill us. Remember?"

"Besides, she's a cat. She could have killed her

instead. Now Lacy gets to live out a simple, stress free existence," Blake pointed out, keeping his voice down.

"Lacy? Was that her name?" Merideth demanded loudly, ignoring their magister's request.

"It was. I thought of that myself," Blake teased, his finger waving around in the air as if he were rearranging the letters. "Lacy…Caly. Pretty clever, huh?"

"You're such a dick," Rider stepped in. "You can't take a person and turn them into a cat."

"Well, apparently you can," Sarah snipped, placing her hands on her hips.

"Sarah," Merideth hissed.

"You should change her back," Joseline pushed.

"Oh, no," Sarah bit angrily, ready to defend herself. "She was evil, and she definitely got what she deserved."

"Besides, that spell is irreversible. She's stuck," Karen added.

Closing his eyes, Blake pinched the bridge of his nose, shaking his head slowly. "Oh, you kids! You are going to be the death of me!"

"Kids?" Rider echoed, looking around. "Are you referring to us?"

"Yeah, you!" Blake looked up, swinging around within their huddle. "You are all kids to me, acting like a bunch of children! I told you this isn't the place to have this discussion!" His voice raised, a few people stared, but most were too busy with their own lives to give them a second glance.

"Well, it's fine now," Meri pointed out, indicating the gate. "It's our turn to board." Picking up her bag, she marched towards the entrance. Presenting her pass, she left them behind as she headed down the tube and onto the plane.

Locating their seats in their customary first class, she cornered one of the attendants. "I need a gray-goose martini as soon as we are in the air, please. And, uh… keep them coming."

Overhearing her, Sarah choked. "Is she seriously getting sloshed?" She didn't think the cat incident was *that* bad.

"She must really hate to fly," Karen commented with a giggle. "Where are our seats?"

"Actually, these are our seats," Blake informed her, indicating the oversized recliners with an open palm. "Apparently, Madam Monroe only flies first class."

"No way!" Sarah squealed. "Do we get caviar?"

Blake laughed, shaking his head. "I doubt it. And we're not sitting together, so I have a small favor to ask."

"Like what," Sarah demanded, eyeing him warily.

"Can you two sit together? I'd like to partner with Joseline." He leaned closer to them, whispering loudly. "Do a little recruiting." He winked for good measure.

The girls exchanged a short look, then nodded. "I can sit with her. But be nice to my girlfriend," Karen instructed.

"No worries." Blake clamped her on the shoulder, then turned in the narrow aisle. "Oh Joseline," he sang, working his way over to her. "We're here." He pointed out two seats for them.

"Oh. I assumed I would sit with Karen."

"Well, I was hoping to give those two a little time to work on their disagreement," he explained, again using a loud whisper.

"Ah, that makes sense. Ok, but I get the window." She didn't wait for conformation and slipped into the preferred seat.

"No problem." He flopped down next to her, shoving his pack underneath.

"You travel light," she observed.

"What does a man need besides clean underwear and a spot of gel for his hair?"

He grinned, genuinely glad to have some alone time with her.

"Well, I hope you brought a few more things than that," she teased. "Bad breath can be a real turnoff."

"Yeah, you got me there." He winced, not sure she found him as suave as he felt. Giving it a break, he waited until they were in the air before he pushed on. "Listen, Joseline, I was actually hoping to speak to you as well."

"I'm in," she replied shortly, staring at an article in the inflight magazine.

"What? You're in?" He scrunched his brow, turning to look at her profile. "I haven't even told you what it's about."

Closing the glossy pages, she gave him a sly smile. "I assume it's about the coven."

"Yeah." His features relaxed. "You want to be a part of us, then?"

"Oh, absolutely." She chuckled, noting the attendant. "Can I get a dry sherry, please?"

"And for you sir?" the thin blonde asked.

"Uh, a beer. Doesn't matter what kind. Thanks."

Waiting until she had gone another set of chairs, Joseline leaned against Blake's arm. "I love you guys. Of course I'm willing to throw in with you."

"You do realize Rider and Merideth aren't really with us," he cautioned.

"I know. But there's hope yet. And I'm not going to New Orleans with them, no matter how fabulous it is. I've already built a life in Boston. My shop and my adoptive family is there," she pointed out solemnly. "So is Karen."

"You really like her, huh?" He accepted his beverage, then passed hers to her.

"I do!" She scrunched her face into a happy grin. "And if it doesn't work out, that's ok. We will be great friends, either way."

"Have you spoken to Hubert?" he dared, unsure how she felt about that part of her life under current circumstances.

"No, I've been sending his calls to voicemail and flat ignoring the texts. I'll call him when we get back in town," she explained, keeping it short. "I need to figure out a few things before I confront them."

"Confront." He coughed. "They really did us a favor, taking you in. I hope you're not too hard on them."

"I won't be." She laughed at his literal translation. "Thanks, Blake. I can tell you're going to be a fabulous magister."

"Well, that makes one of us." He toyed with his drink. "It's harder than I thought it would be. I can do magic with my eyes closed. But this?" He turned in his seat, looking around the cabin. A seat ahead of them and on the other side, Rider and Meri appeared to be passed out. A few seats back across the aisle, Karen and Sarah were talking non-stop. "Keeping up with other people is a lot of work."

"Yes. You're the boss. You can't really be friends with us. Even your relationship with Sarah will cause potential problems."

"My relationship—" he snapped around to face her, "what's that got to do with anything?"

"She's beneath you. And not just in bed. With you in charge, you have to run things. You can't play favorites, and she won't always get her way," Joseline explained. "And just so we are square, she really should put Lacy back. I'm going to help her if I can."

"I know. And she knows that. You would go against me if I said she needs to stay on four legs?" Blake huffed, suddenly feeling less in charge than he had when they sat down.

"No. If you make that call, I will honor it. I know my place. But if you value our opinions, and I hope you do, that's mine."

Puckering his lips, he stewed, then asked, "Does anyone else know? About your 'other' talent? Besides talking to cat-witches." He chuckled at his little joke.

Cutting her eyes up at him, she grinned. "Very good. Karen has figured it out, but the rest, I don't think they have a clue."

"Good. Probably best if they don't know. I'm sure it would make them a little uncomfortable around you. Meri already makes it a bit tense at times." He nodded, the wheels turning. "But that does leave us with a few possibilities. How would you like to be my spy? Let me know how things are going once in a while."

"I'd like that." She grinned deviously. "You are really something, Blake Korrigan."

"I try." Hoisting his beer, he drank, letting her go back to her reading in peace.

To Talk About

IT WAS WELL after nine that night when the weary group pulled into the Monroe driveway. Climbing out of the driver's side, Rider stretched in an exaggerated fashion. Stepping out of the sliding door behind him, Blake cracked him on the back. "Thanks for driving, man. I'd have taken a turn if you had let me."

"It wasn't that far," Rider shot back, returning the clap to his shoulder. "You can drive home."

Blake nodded, noting the other man didn't say whether or not he would be present for that trip. They had brought all their things, so as the saying goes, they didn't leave anything in Boston.

The door to the house opened and the drive area flooded with bright light. "Meri, is that you?"

"Of course it is, Daddy." She ran to her father, flinging herself into his arms. "I found her," she whispered as he squeezed. "I hope that's ok."

"Absolutely." He rocked her side to side, extending the hug as the others gathered suitcases and made their way to the open doorway. Releasing her, Garrett chuckled. "Well, isn't this a ragged bunch." He offered his hand to Blake. "It's been a while, son."

"You know him?" Rider gasped, confused by the connection. "If you guys knew who helped to hide Joseline, why didn't you just tell us that to begin with? We could have left my father out of this completely."

Garrett's features twisted, and he tried to hold the smile, failing miserably. "I wasn't aware of that," he stated, his tone a little less friendly.

"Sorry, Garrett." Blake kicked the ground. "If it hadn't been May that asked, I never would have gotten involved."

"It's quite all right, Judoc. I'm sure that brother of yours had a hand in it as well." Garrett's forgiveness sounded sincere.

"Actually, I'm Blake now. And you know he did." Stepping closer, he gave Garrett's arm a squeeze. His voice low, his words only for him, he added, "We have much to discuss, old friend."

"Later," Garrett agreed. "We'll get the kids to bed, then we'll talk." Turning to Meri, his eyes moved past her, noticing the wayward sister behind her. "Well, I'll be damned." His brown orbs darting between them, he observed, "The two of you could have been twins."

"We are pretty close," Joseline agreed. Coming forward, she offered her hand. "This crew calls me Josee, so I guess that will have to do."

Shaking her hand, Garrett's expression drifted into hard to read. "If I had known how much the two of you would resemble, I might have insisted on raising you myself. But, then again, that wasn't really my call."

"It's ok," she reassured. "I'm here now. Can I see my mother?"

Garrett's features grew pained. "I'll show you inside, but you should prepare yourself. Both of you." He glanced at Meri. "She's taken a bad turn. I think we are down to days."

"Where is she?" Merideth breathed.

"We've set up a hospital bed in the den," her father explained. "She's comfortable in there. She's been waiting for you."

The two girls didn't hesitate, dropping their bags in the foyer and rushing into the dimly lit room where Ezamay lay. Each taking a side, they claimed a hand.

"Mother," Meri gently called. "I found your Joseline."

Her eyes fluttering, the older woman looked between them. The girls might have fooled a stranger, but she could easily tell them apart. "Oh, my Meri. Joseline, you said?" She turned her head, giving the other girl a squeeze.

"Call me Josee, Mom." Her eyes filled with tears, then brimmed over to stain her cheeks. "I always knew I had another home."

"You do, my darling." Ezamay wheezed. "You have one whenever you should like to have it."

Bending, Joseline raised the wrinkled hand, caressing it with a moist cheek. "I wish I had known sooner. I have so much to ask. So much to tell!"

After kissing the other hand, which she still held, Meri lay it on her mother's chest. "I'll go join the others. You two deserve some time."

At the door, the group hovered, unsure whether to

enter or find another room to congregate in. "Judoc's here." Ezamay noticed his tall profile.

"Yes, he came with us. Only we call him Blake now." Meri giggled anxiously, unsure how to label their relationship. Everything had become so muddled since she left her mother's house in search of her sibling a few weeks before. "Do you wish to speak to him? I'll send him over."

Leaving the railing, Meri rushed over to the group. "Mother wishes to see you, Blake."

"Not now. Later, perhaps. Let Joseline have a few moments to herself. Let's get coffee or something, shall we?" he suggested, hoping to keep their spirits up.

Glancing back at the pair, Meri smiled. Joseline had taken a seat on a tall stool, probably placed there by her father. Still clasping the tired hand, she held it fondly, the two women talking and nodding, with the occasional smile. "Ok, we'll get some refreshments. It's this way."

Guiding them down the hall, the group arrived in a huge, yet immaculate, kitchen. The center held a large island and a row of bar stools ran down the back side.

"Oh, this place is incredible," Sarah observed. Claiming one of the giant seats, she beamed. "Could you imagine having this to dine in every night?"

Meri laughed. "We didn't eat in here. This area is for preparing meals. The dining room is down the hall."

"Fancy," Karen observed, also taking a stool. "We would have so much room. Ours is so small."

Merideth swallowed, her features drawn. "Your place isn't small, it's cozy."

Blake cut his eyes over at her as Rider located the coffee pot. "You will miss us, I think," he said quietly.

"We'll miss our sister, I know that," Rider replied, pushing buttons, then cursing. "How do you work this damn thing?" After a few more tries, he gave up. "It's too much for me."

At that moment, an older woman entered the room. Glancing around at the group, she appeared calm and ready to serve them.

"Oh, Alice, you needn't have come. We would have been fine," Meri rebuked her.

"And my kitchen would have been a mess." Shooing Rider away from the device, she pointed at the table. "Take a seat and I will have coffee for you in no time."

"Thanks," he replied, bowing before slipping away. Selecting a chair at the table, he folded his hands, twiddling his thumbs while he waited.

When the coffee was served, they each gathered a cup and joined him. As they settled into the cushioned chairs, Sarah mumbled, "Will we get a room soon? Some of us didn't sleep on the plane."

"Forgive me. I've been a terrible hostess. I can have Alice show you where you and Blake will sleep," Meri offered.

"Will Joseline and I share a room?" Karen looked hopeful. "I bet she stays with her mother, though, if she can."

"I would plan on bunking alone," Rider agreed. "She'll want every minute she can get."

"She will have to share at some point, though. I do need to speak with May as soon as possible." Blake glanced at the clock on the wall. "It's just after ten. I'd say they get another half hour, and then I'm going in."

"What could possibly be so important?" Sarah demanded sharply. "You'll see her in the morning."

"I can't risk it." Blake sipped his brew. "May needs to hear what I have to say, and then we can all get some sleep." Glancing between the two women, he frowned. "Actually, you guys might as well go to bed. The rest of us will be up for quite a while." He raised a brow at Meri, signaling it was time for that escort.

"I may as well turn in, too." Rider yawned for effect.

"It's fine if you go, but you might like to be part of the discussion."

"And what exactly are you discussing?" Sarah asked, her interest piqued.

"Old business. Nothing that would really affect you," Blake assured.

"Alice, can you show the girls to a couple of rooms? They'll be going to bed soon." Meri's request earned a simple nod. "Thank you."

"Wow. Sending the kids off to bed so the grownups can talk," Karen teased. Out of her chair, she followed the housekeeper nonetheless, each picking up their bags in the foyer to haul up the stairs.

"Aren't you leaving?" Blake flicked his gaze to Rider.

"I'll go in a minute. I know which room is ours." Rider caught his stare and lowered his voice. "Or is this something I really need to hear."

"We need to discuss Morcant." Blake kept his voice low, as if he were afraid to mention his brother at full volume.

"Now?" Merideth wrinkled her nose.

"Yes," Blake hissed. "It is vital that we share his actions with May. Tonight, if at all possible."

"Maybe I should stay up for this," Rider growled. Looking over his shoulder, he too assessed the clock. "About twenty more minutes, right?"

"Yeah. We'll give them that, but then we have to push on," Blake determined.

"Why do I get the feeling we've just been sent to the kid's table?" Karen groused as she followed the maid to the second floor.

Sarah shrugged, trudging beside her. "What do we care? This doesn't really concern either of us."

Karen looked over her shoulder, back down the stairs. "I guess you're right."

"These are your rooms," Alice informed them, pointing at doorways across from each other.

"Thanks." Sarah smiled, wondering if they should tip her, like a bellhop. "Well, that answers that," she observed as the older woman retreated.

"Answers what?" Karen asked, inspecting the equally sparse chambers. "Jos and I'll take this one." She stepped in, dropping their bags on the floor to claim it.

"Just a random thought." Sarah dismissed her question. "Are you going to sleep?"

"Not likely. You want to hang out a while?" Karen asked eagerly, happy they had mended their quarrel on the plane.

"I can." Sarah tossed the bags she had carried into the other room, then had a look around the one Karen had chosen. Noting the lack of seats, she opted for the bed, stretching across it sideways. Lying on her back, she sighed. "I'm sorry I got all pissy about you and Josee. It really isn't my place to judge."

"It's ok." Karen took the opposite direction, so they were head to feet of each other. "I've given you a lot of grief lately. I'm the one who should apologize."

"Are you still moving back to Atlanta?"

"I dunno," Karen slurred. "I feel like I was only making the move to run away."

"Morcant's in prison," Sarah reminded her.

"Not from him." Karen paused, curling her tongue. "I was running away from you."

"From me?!" Sarah sat straight up, glaring at her. "What did I do?"

"Nothing." Karen cut her eyes over at her from the reclined position. "I didn't want to face you. After the way I acted and insisted you couldn't tell anyone."

"Couldn't tell anyone what?" Sarah's voice softened. "You're my best friend. We've more or less lived four houses away from each other our entire lives."

"I know, but that night I made you promise not to tell. It would make me a hypocrite if I changed my mind."

"You're talking about that night we…" Sarah's voice trailed away.

"Yeah, and the shower. All of it." Karen inhaled deeply, then blew the air out in a steady stream. "Didn't you ever wonder? I always collected a swarm of boys, all vying for my attention. But a few dates and it was over. I was never really into any of them."

"I was so jealous of how easily you attracted them," Sarah confessed, leaning back against stiff arms.

"Well, don't be." Karen sat up next to her. "I like

girls. It was a real bitch move of me that night to deny it, and I will always regret it."

Sarah's brow furrowed, her mind racing. Lost for words, her lips parted, emitting a low hiss. "Oh, Karen."

"I should have made love to you. I wanted to, but I didn't. I will always wish I had." Karen's voice cracked, her bottom lip quivering.

"But that's not true! I was possessed, remember? Take off your rose-colored glasses, Karen. I practically raped you!" Sarah's eyes grew misty. Falling against each other, they folded into a strong embrace. "And now you have Joseline. You really like her, don't you?" Sarah released her grip, leaning back to study her best friend. "Or is it just a fling?"

"I adore her." Karen let go as well and shifted to grab the box of tissues from the nightstand. Sharing them, she added, "We have a connection I just can't explain."

"You're not moving back to Atlanta," Sarah concluded.

"No, probably not." Karen grinned. "I am going for a visit after graduation, though. I want to take Jos and show her off. And speaking of graduation, did you bring your laptop? I forgot about a paper I have to turn in by Thursday."

Sarah gasped, looking around her. "Do you think we will be here that long?"

Following her thoughts, Karen chuckled. "Afraid you two might have to take a few nights off?"

Sarah's gaze snapped to meet hers.

"Come on, I know when you guys get it on. You rock the whole house!"

"We do not rock the house," Sarah denied, then

faltered. "Do we?"

"Yeah. I get a blow by blow from pretty much anywhere but my room, since it's so far away from yours."

"Shit." Sarah flushed. "I guess that old crone didn't get all of Brenna out of me."

"It's ok," Karen soothed. "Blake's a hot guy and he really was a womanizer, just like Joseline said, which makes you perfect together. I'm just surprisede he hasn't gotten you knocked up already."

The color in Sarah's cheeks deepened. "I'm not ready for a baby. Blake and I have an agreement."

"Oh?" Karen clipped, pursing her lips. "But you've wanted them ever since I can remember. You will later, right?"

"That was before." Sarah tossed her red hair, considering her dilemma. "If I tell him I'm not ready yet, he fucks me in the ass." She paused, then added, "He thinks he's punishing me."

Karen's brows went up. "Is he punishing you?"

"No." Sarah giggled. "I. Love. It. I'm terrified he won't do it anymore if I agree to get pregnant."

Karen gaped at her. "You know that's probably not true. He isn't punishing you; he adores you. If you told him that's what you wanted, Blake would do anything for you."

Sarah sighed. "I believe that, too. But if I'm wrong, I don't know what I would do. How did we get from talking about Joseline to my ass anyway?"

"Oh, Sarah!" Karen broke into a rolling laugh before tamping it down. "I hope we will always be best friends who can talk about anything."

NINETEEN

Time to Fight

AS SOON AS the women left the kitchen in search of sleeping quarters, Blake announced, "We don't have much time."

"Time for what?" Merideth asked, following him out of the room with Rider trailing behind them. Arriving at the den, he waited for her. "Blake, what is going on?"

"I'm only going to explain it once. Are you coming in so everyone can hear, or joining the others upstairs?" He glanced between them, waiting impatiently for them to decide.

"You're making such a big deal," Rider chided. "If it's that important, why would you exclude them?"

"Sarah and Karen both suffered deeply at my brother's hand. I do not wish to involve them unless we have to," Blake clipped.

"What does Morcant have to do with my mother?" Meri whispered, afraid Ezamay or Josee would overhear them.

"I don't know yet," Blake clarified. "That's what we

need to discuss." Turning, he led the way into the dimly lit room.

"I hear you are Blake now," Ezamay greeted him, extending her hand.

"Yes. A symbol of my altered persona," he explained, folding his fingers around her weathered palm. "My dear May," he said more quietly. "I have missed you so."

"It has been too long," she agreed. "Thank you for taking such good care of my daughter." She glanced at the girl still seated beside her. "She informs me she will be part of your coven."

"Indeed." Blake adjusted the blanket across her bosom, resting her hand on top of it. "I will be honored to have her."

At the foot of the oversized bed, Meri and Rider fidgeted.

"Is something wrong?" Blake squared himself, forming a circle of sorts with the others.

"We were not aware of that decision," Merideth admitted quietly.

"Don't you people ever sleep?" Garrett interrupted from the doorway. "Ezamay needs her rest."

"I'll rest when I'm dead," she replied hoarsely.

"Care to join us?" Blake called to him. "We were just about to discuss May's condition."

"What about her condition?" Garrett sidled in next Joselin, with Rider on his left.

"I have concerns." Blake shoved his hands in his pockets. "I find this fast-moving cancer unnatural."

"Are you suggesting my wife is cursed?" Garrett spat.

"I think we should explore the possibility," Blake countered.

"Who would care to curse an old woman like me?" Ezamay quipped, fighting to sit up.

"Here, Mother. We need to raise the head." Meri scooted around, searching for the button.

"I've got it." Joseline pressed the switch and the motor hummed.

Next to her, Blake leaned in and adjusted her pillow. When he had made her comfortable, he hovered close. "I'm sorry, May, but I fear my brother has done this to you."

Ezamay gasped. "But Morcant is my friend!"

"He cursed me as well," Joseline confessed. Pulling the chain around her neck, she held up the amulet. "And I'm not the only one. You saw Sarah?"

"Which one is she?" Ezamay wheezed, then coughed. "I wasn't properly introduced."

"The tall red-head," Blake informed her.

"Who used to be a much shorter and rounder brunet," Josee added.

"How'd you know that?" Blake blinked at her.

"Karen still has some photographs. We spent some time walking down memory lane the other night." She grinned, recalling what else they had done.

"Oh." His lips puckered. "Yes, he cursed Sarah, but for a darker purpose." His face lost three shades of color, and he looked up at the ceiling. "The vessel still waits."

"What vessel? Blake, what the hell are you talking about?" Garrett growled.

"Sarah," he breathed. Lowering his eyes to the woman before him, he shook his head slowly. "Even from prison he is making our lives hell."

"That's it. I'm going to bed. And I suggest the rest of

you do the same!" Garrett waved at them over his shoulder as he left the room.

"You're going to have to explain," Merideth prodded. "What does my mother's illness have to do with Morcant?"

"He is consumed by darkness and obsessed with Brenna," Blake began. "He is convinced he can bring her back from the dead through a curse she made before she was crucified for witchcraft over five-hundred-years ago."

"An old witch's tale." Ezamay chuckled. "What rubbish."

"Did you see her hair? And what my mother pulled out of her— he froze, his eyes darting around at the others. "Shit. I hope she hid it somewhere safe."

"Hid what?" Rider demanded, tempted to take his own tired ass to bed. "Seriously, man, you are talking in riddles and it's too fucking late for that shit."

"After Morcant cursed her, Sarah began a transformation. I took her to see my mother. She's an old crone. Very powerful. She extracted Brenna from her and placed her in a vessel. I fear this curse on May is some play to get at it," Blake explained in as short a way as he could. Glancing at the others, he assessed if it had been enough.

Joseline's jaw dropped. "If that's true, all we have to do to save her is to extract the curse!"

"It's not that easy," Blake lamented, shaking his head. "First, we have to have the spell he used."

"Or a good counter measure," Garrett called from the door.

"I thought you were going to bed!" Blake taunted.

Ignoring him, Garrett wandered into the room, stopping halfway to the group. "Your mother may be the most powerful witch I have ever known. She couldn't destroy her? Brenna, I mean?"

"I don't know if it was a couldn't or wouldn't. Morcant was always her favorite, so the fact that she helped us at all surprised the hell out of me," Blake confessed, running his fingers through his dark hair.

"What would we need to do?" Meri asked quietly. "If we wanted to counter his curse, or whatever?"

"Well, I have an entire bookstore full of texts. If we were at home, I'd start hunting for the spell, or one likely to have caused this strange illness," he explained calmly.

"But we aren't at your shop. We're here. Hey!" Rider snapped. "Meri and I found quite a bit of useful stuff online when we were on the run."

"And we visited the tuath," she added. "Maybe there's one of those around here who could help us."

Garrett cleared his throat. "I doubt you would find anyone at this hour, but if you care to follow me, I might be able to help."

"Unlikely, but what the hell," Blake muttered as the four friends followed him down the hall.

In his study, Garrett stopped in the center of the room, spreading his arms to indicate the wall-to-wall bookcase that covered the back. "My collection is in here."

"These are nice, but we need magic books," Rider pointed out.

Reaching the shelves in a few steps, Garrett grasped the front of the case, pulling firmly. A section of the wall gave way, sliding towards him. Grasping one end, he shoved it aside, revealing a second layer of tomes. Turning to the group, he indicated his collection. "When I came of age, I swore I would never touch the craft, and to this day I have kept my word."

"You're a witch, Daddy?" Merideth gaped at him. Her intuition had never given so much as a hint of such a thing.

"Of course. Your mother was promised to me by her father, I'm sure in some plot to draw me into the coven," he explained, glancing at their solemn faces.

"But you don't practice." Rider rocked his jaw. "Like us."

"Oh, no. Like you." Garrett pointed at him with a stiff digit. "Merideth has been practicing since she was ten years old." He shrugged. "Even if I wanted to keep her out of the magical world, she was born to it."

"My intuitions," she whispered. "It was real!"

"Yes, very real." Her father nodded. "That's one reason I agreed to be the keeper of our family's library as the elders passed on. When I realized you would be a wielder of magic, despite my wishes, I knew that one day they would be yours."

"Like Mother's diary." Meri pressed her lips together, forming a small grin. "I had no idea."

"Your mother's gift to you was only the beginning. Here, you will find hundreds, even thousands of spells, all passed down through our line. And now they are yours." With that, he headed for the door.

"Where are you going?" Blake demanded. "We have to find the spell."

"No, you have to find it," Garrett clipped. "I told you, I have never touched the craft, and I will not break my vow."

"Not even for your wife? For Meri's mother?" Rider bit angrily.

"Not even for that which I hold most dear," Garrett agreed. "I'll check on you in the morning." And with that, he left them to their find.

"So, what do we do now?" Joseline asked, at a loss.

"We search," Blake suggested, pulling down one of the large texts. "We should get the others. We will need every pair of eyes we can get." The book fell open on the desk before him, and he grunted. "Please tell me you two read Gaelic."

Rider began to laugh. "We're non-practicing." His smile fading, he added, "We'll take ours in English, thanks."

"They don't come in English." Joseline offered the book she had opened. "I bet they are all the same."

Pulling out her phone, Merideth snapped a picture of a page, then giggled. "Google translates." She held out the device. "Like magic."

"Haha," Blake taunted, twisting the screen so he could see it. "Hey, that's not bad!"

"How do I get that?" Joseline demanded, eager to save their mother.

"I'll show you. Rider, where's your phone?" Meri looked up at him, and he didn't bother to argue.

"I'll get the girls. You guys get started. We need a stack of possibles. Anything that looks promising, mark, and I'll take a look at it," Blake instructed as he left the room.

The following morning, Garrett wandered into his den, coffee mug in hand. "Wow. You guys have been busy."

"Yeah." Rider answered, but no one looked up. "I may have another one."

"Put it on the desk and I'll get to it," Blake promised.

Meandering around, Garrett inspected the books each of them were working on, then made his way to the desk. Several tomes were open with spells exposed. "Oh, this one is nice. Blake, we should try this one."

"We still have a few more tomes to look through," the magister informed him. He looked up to see the owner of the house appeared fully rested. "Sleep well?"

"Indeed, I did." Taking a noisy slurp, he pushed. "I know I said I wouldn't use the craft, but I will help. Let's try this transference." He indicated his favorite of the lot.

"That spell won't work," Blake clipped, returning to his reading. "It requires another person to be sacrificed."

"I said, I'll do it," Garratt said more forcefully.

Meri looked up at her father. "You'll do what, Daddy?"

"I'll take your mother's curse. I'll be the sacrifice." He drank again, calmly, as if he were talking about lunch.

Slapping his pages together, Blake stood. "I can't let you do that."

"You don't have a choice." Garrett tapped him on the chest with a stiff digit. "We've been friend's a long time. You know I would do anything for May."

"Yeah, but sacrificing your own life?"

"We don't have time to argue. Or spend any more time hunting. If there was another way, you would have found it. Let's do this, before it's too late." Garrett's word's persuasive, the others closed their books in turn and joined them.

"What do we have to do to use the spell?" Joseline asked tentatively. "I've never actually cast one before."

"We need a good caster," Garrett pointed out. "Blake's decent, but this has to be perfect."

The rest turned in unison, focusing on Sarah.

"What? Why me?" She shook her long red hair. "This is a lot of responsibility."

"I know a cat who says you'll do great at it," Joseline replied, only half joking.

"A cat?" Garrett's brows raised.

"Long story." Blake dismissed his quarry, handing the book to Sarah. "Go practice. We'll get Ezamay ready."

"And the room," Karen added. "Everything must be in place."

Sarah glared at the page. "Not in the den. Go prep the kitchen. You can put May on that giant island in there."

"Oh, my. Alice isn't going to like that," Merideth observed.

"Fuck Alice," Rider barked. "A woman's life is at stake."

"Go work on the spell." Blake shooed Sarah out, then turned to the rest of them. "Let's go prep the kitchen. I want to be ready to go when she is."

TWENTY

Practiced Hands

THE GROUP STORMED into the kitchen, each inspecting the furnishings with new eyes. "These will need to go," Blake observed. Catching a stool in each hand, he placed them next to a wall.

Alice greeted them from her position at the stove. "I'll have breakfast for you shortly." Looking around at their odd behavior, she added, "What is going on?"

"Breakfast can wait," Blake clipped, moving the remaining two seats from the bar. "Sarah's right. This island in here is perfect." He leaned on the top of it, testing his weight against it. "If you can find me a Sharpie, I'll mark it for the ritual."

Alice gasped. "What on earth?"

Stepping between them, Garrett addressed the house-keeper firmly. "We've had a change in plans. How about you take the day off?"

"The day off? With so many mouths to feed?" She looked around, bewildered as to their rummaging around her workspace so blatantly.

"Yes. We're going to have a little get together and we won't be needing food," her boss explained. "I'm giving you the day off. Please tell Polly and Jackson they are excused, as well."

The housekeeper looked as if she might argue, so Merideth joined her father's cause. "Really Alice. It's a surprise for Mother. Be a dear and let the others know on your way out."

Glancing between them, Alice shrugged. "Ok, if that's the way you want it." Pulling the strings of her apron as she exited the room, she mumbled to herself until she was out of sight.

"What do we need?" Merideth asked, turning to Blake.

"Candles," Joseline suggest.

"Yes, and lots of them," Blake agreed. "Too bad those stools have cushioned tops, or we could use them to set them on."

"I'll go through the house and gather any small tables I can find," Karen offered.

"I can run get candles, if they're that important." Rider turned his palms out in doubt.

"We won't pull this off without them," Blake informed him. "Their energy helps fuel the spell. Like life itself embodied within each tiny flame."

"Morcant must have been a prolific caster," Joseline teased. "He was one of our biggest customers at the Broken Match."

"What kind did he buy?" Rider turned to her. "I want to get this right."

"It shouldn't matter, should it Blake?" She deferred to his judgement.

"Not in a pinch. Get whatever you can, as many as you can, and be quick about it," Blake instructed, his mind still on clearing the room.

"Are there any candle shops in town?" Rider asked, tugging on his coat.

"Google is your friend," Merideth teased, stealing a kiss as he made is exit.

"Right. Google has really saved our asses this trip." Leaving by the front door, he pulled out his phone and made the search, heading out of the driveway a few minutes later.

"I found this for you." Garrett returned from his study and handed Blake a marker, then watched as he used it to draw an oversized pentagram that covered the beautiful tile top from side to side.

"I want to put a pallet up here," Blake suggested when he had finished. "Ezamay may have to lay there for a while. I have no idea how long the cast will take."

"I'll gather some blankets and make a pallet," Meri informed him, taking the hall and the stairs to the bedrooms above.

"Joseline, I have a special chore for you," Blake said quietly, catching her by the arm. "Go and sit with your mother. Keep her talking, or let her rest, but please don't let her catch wind of what is going on."

"Why not?"

"We need her to be relaxed. To want to let the curse leave her. If she discovers our plan, it may not work," he concluded.

"I'll try. But don't we have to tell her something?" she pointed out. "We can't just bring her in here and perform the ritual without expecting her to notice."

SAMANTHA JACOBEY

"Fine, but keep it simple. Tell her we have found a way to extract the curse, but nothing else," he commanded firmly.

"Yes, sir." She walked slowly towards the den, considering what she would say. She never had been much of a liar, so she would need a plan if she wanted to sound convincing.

Watching her go, Blake shook his head.

"What else do we need?" Garrett asked from over his shoulder.

"A miracle," Blake whispered. "I'm not convinced this will work."

"May's life depends on it." Garrett came around to his side, leaning close to keep the conversation between them. "You'll look out for her when I'm gone, right?"

"We all will." Blake cut his eyes over at him. "I can't believe you never told Meri...anything."

"Why would I? Ezamay and I agreed long ago that this would be a non-magical house. She gave up the craft for me," he concluded.

"She loves you very much, my friend. Don't ever think she married you because her father chose you."

"Thanks, Blake. I'm sure she does." Garrett's eyes grew misty. "Talk about something else, dammit."

"Well, we need to decide how we are going to transport her. Can she walk?" Blake's features appeared doubtful.

"I'll carry her," Garrett stated confidently.

"All right. Why don't you see how Karen is coming with the tables? We need to fill this room with light." He grinned at the thought of it.

"Right. I can't wait to see Alice when she walks in

tomorrow." Garrett laughed at the thought as he strolled away to accomplish his new task.

Shaking his head, Blake also chuckled.

"What's so funny?" Merideth asked, returning with the blankets and a pillow for her head.

"Just something your father said about Alice." He turned to help her with the pallet. "I need to mark the floor before we put this together."

"The floor?" She looked at him, wrinkling her nose.

"So everyone will know where to stand. Sarah may be the caster, but this will be a team effort."

"I don't have much experience with any of this." Meri sighed.

"I'm sorry for that." He could tell by her motions that her mood had fallen. "Your father was speculating about Alice's reaction when she comes in tomorrow. Do you think she'll be mad?"

"Furious. It will be quite the show," she assured him, her features softening. "I hope he's here tomorrow to see it."

At that moment, Karen returned with a pair of small tables. "Where do you want them?"

"Everywhere. Start lining the edges of the room with them. And pull the pictures and stuff down off the walls. We don't want anything above them that might catch fire."

Working steadily, the group had the kitchen nearly in order by the time Rider returned. "Where have you been?" Blake snapped as soon as he entered their converted space.

"Buying candles, where else?" Rider shot back. "Want to help carry them in?"

"Did you get enough?" Meri asked, following close behind them.

"If I didn't, then there aren't enough to be had. Period." He chortled at his own joke. Opening the back of the van, he exposed the stacks of boxes.

"Wow," Karen breathed. "Yeah, that ought to do it." She grabbed a case off the top and headed back inside. Each of the group followed suit, leaving a few that would need a second trip.

"Open them and start setting them out," Blake instructed.

"Shouldn't we put them on plates?" Merideth asked, inspecting a case of tall, tapered ones. "To catch the dripping wax?"

"Man, your housekeeper is going to love us," he growled. "Yeah, plates will be ok, but be quick about it. Drop a bit of wax onto the plate to seat the candle, and they should work great. I'll go see how Sarah is doing." When he reached the den, he paused, peeking in at the mother and daughter, deep in conversation. Drawn to them, he let Sarah be a bit longer and stepped inside. "You two ok in here?"

"We're just waiting for the party." Ezamay beamed. "Josee tells me you found the right spell. You can cure me!"

"Yes, well, we are going to remove the curse. I don't really know how long the healing will take. We're going to give it our best shot, May." He stopped at the foot of her bed. "You keep your spirits up and we'll get started as soon as we can." He squeezed her foot affectionately, then fled the room.

On the stairs, he took them as rapidly as he could, but

when he arrived at their room, Sarah was nowhere to be found. "Sarah?" he called, stomping down the hall and checking room by room.

"I'm in here!" Her voice sounded far away.

"Where? This damn house is too fucking big," he groaned, reminded of his own family dwelling.

"The master suite," she clarified.

"The master suite?!" he echoed. "What the hell are you doing in here? Ooh." He moaned, enchanted by her appearance.

"You like?" She grinned, turning to model the long white gown she had discovered.

"It looks great. But why?"

"I wanted to dress for the occasion," she clipped, handing him the book. "Are we ready downstairs?" She brushed past him, swaying her arms as she walked to enjoy the feel of the flowing sleeves that hung to the tips of her fingers.

"Ready when you are," he agreed, following her down the hall, pressing the ancient tome to his chest.

When they arrived at the kitchen, the place was almost unrecognizable. "Wow," she breathed. "I love what you've done with the place." Every available inch held a flickering flame. "Where did you find so many candles?" She turned slowly to admire the wide range of colors.

"I practically cleared out a craft shop," Rider informed her, stacking the last two cases next to the door. "I have a few left if you see where we can fit them."

"No, this is great!" She flicked off the overhead lights. "Amazing, really." She twirled, causing the dress to poof out around her, enjoying the feel of the energy flow around her.

"What the hell!" Merideth grunted. "You went in my mother's closet?"

Stopping the spin, Sarah faced her, a little dizzy she swayed. "It felt right," she defended quietly, noticing Garrett in the hallway behind her, Ezamay in his arms. She ran her hands anxiously over the silky material, wondering what its owner would say.

When they cleared the door, the matriarch squealed. "Put me down, Garrett!"

Placing her bare feet on the tile floor, he helped her to stand. "Easy, May."

Spreading her arms, Ezamay grinned. "You must be Sarah. And how lovely you look!" Reaching her, she clasped her hands. "They tell me you are a very talented caster."

Sarah shifted her weight, anxious at the praise. "I hear that, too."

"You don't agree?" The older woman held the smile.

Her cheeks flushed, the girl nodded. "I guess I do."

Looking her up and down, Ezamay sighed. "That dress is yours. It fits you beautifully. I want you to have it when you go home."

"Thank you. I'm sorry I didn't ask. I was working on the spell and I wanted to feel closer to you. When I saw it, I had to try it on." She caressed the fine white material, enjoying it against her skin. "I believe it connects us."

"And so it does." Her movement slow, purposeful, Ezamay pulled the girl into a firm hug. "Thank you for curing my cancer. I will always be grateful."

When she released her, Sarah choked, "Define cure."

"Oh, Sarah!" Blake laughed loudly. "You know what she means." He pivoted to Karen, quickly changing the subject, "Can you help May onto the pallet? I'm sorry, it won't be as cushioned as your bed, but hopefully you won't have to lay there too long."

"It's quite all right. I expect a little discomfort." Taking Karen's hand, Ezamay made the climb on the makeshift steps they had put in place.

Grasping Sarah's arm roughly, Blake guided her away. "Be careful. You can't tell her about Garrett."

"She doesn't know what we're doing?" Sarah hissed. "We can't lie to her about this!"

"It's Garrett's choice. He wants us to save her."

Sarah crossed her arms, biting angrily, "But we shouldn't do it if she wouldn't want us to."

"Like Lacy had a choice," he tossed back, lifting his chin.

Her mouth dropped open, then clamped shut. "It wasn't like that."

"No, it was much worse. Just remember, Garrett will never touch the craft. Ezamay will make a much better ally should we ever need one," he pointed out, glancing around at the others.

"That's cold, Blake," she informed him tartly.

"We're both cold when we have to be," he replied more gently. Leaning down, he kissed her. "Good luck." Spinning, he called to the others, "It's show time, people. Everyone has a mark on the floor where you need to stand. I know for some of you this is your first time, so I'll walk you through it when everyone is in place."

Shuffling to find their names, Garrett moved to stand at Ezamay's head. Placing his hands on her shoulders, he gave her a firm squeeze. "A few more minutes, my sweet."

"I'm fine," she replied, studying him from the odd position. "I'm glad you changed your mind."

"Yes." He lied flatly. "Me, too. But what's the harm in this one time?" He squeezed again, smiling down at her. Joseline had told her that Garrett would be part of the ceremony. However, she had neglected to explain exactly what role he would play. It hurt him that they had lied to her, but he had to ensure that she was cured, no matter the cost.

When everyone had found their assigned location, Blake continued his instructions. "Casting is a simple process. Or for those of us on the star, it will be. Sarah will take on the most difficult portion. When she begins, we all focus. Watch your breathing. In and out, nice and calm. Don't hyperventilate or you'll pass out. Stay on your point and don't move, no matter what happens. Chant if you feel the urge. The more we put into it as a group, the better the outcome will be."

Standing to one side of the star's center, staring down at their patient, Sarah swallowed. Before her, the tome lay open to the spell she had all but memorized. Sliding her fingers over the ancient text, she closed her eyes, hoping her skill would be enough to see it through.

The rest of the group formed a ring, each a point extending the star that Blake had drawn onto the table before the pallet had been lain on top of it. "Ok, this is it, everyone," Sarah informed them, glancing at Karen's shoes as she stood behind her. "All set?" No one dissented. "Here we go."

Placing her hands before her, she pressed the palms

together. Raising her elbows, the sleeves of the dress hung in large swoops of cloth. Her voice low, she chanted the spell, enunciating each syllable. The rhythm came to her easily and a half smiled teased her lips. The energy of the room swirled within her and she could feel it growing.

Reaching the appropriate point, she placed her hands on the torso of Ezamay's prone form. The candles flared, the brightness surrounding them increasing exponentially. Fixated on the chant and the woman before her, she ignored everyone else.

To her right, Merideth fidgeted. They all knew the spell might take a while to complete, but she couldn't stop the waves of worry whirling in her gut. Recalling Blakes instructions, she clenched her fists. Inhaling deeply, she let the breath escape slowly, barely keeping the panic at bay. Catching words and phrases that she recognized, she repeated them quietly to herself in a choppy, haphazard fashion.

To Meri's right stood Blake, who watched her with concerned eyes. When she glanced at him, he frowned. "Focus," he mouthed. Meri nodded, anxiously licking her lips.

Looking to his right, Blake observed Joseline, the opposite of Merideth. Her eyes closed, she breathed deeply and evenly, often repeating portions of the spell. She swayed slightly when a mass of air brushed through the group, her calm unshakable.

Beyond Josee, Rider made the fifth point, with Garrett standing between them, next to the table at Ezamay's head. Garrett maintained his eye-contact with May, never breaking the connection. His hands remained relaxed; despite the fact the casting seemed pure torture.

When Rider's eyes, met Blake's, they held the gaze for several stanzas before Blake slowly closed his pale blue orbs. The air around them stirred again, more forcefully. Bracing himself against it, he waited for the end that would soon come.

"Garrett!" Ezamay screamed, fighting to roll over.

"Don't move!" Blake shouted. "Everyone as you are. Do not break the sphere."

"Garrett," Ezamay sobbed, squirming to free herself. She felt hot, and another gust of air brushed through the group, causing the flames around them to dance wildly.

A few candles were blown over or extinguished, and whisps of smoke trailed up towards the ceiling. Sarah never broke the chant. Raising her voice, she continued, her hands pressing down on the belly beneath her palms, holding Ezamay in place.

"Please, Mother," Merideth quietly begged, wiggling where she stood with the need to go to her. Behind her a candle hissed. She didn't dare turn around to look but feared the wall might be ablaze. Meeting Rider's stare across from her, she realized he wouldn't allow the house to burn down around them and managed to calm herself.

Reaching the end, Sarah's voice grew, forcing the others to repeat her words. Tapping the beat against his leg, Blake again closed his eyes, remaining in position until she shouted the final words, and the room fell silent.

TWENTY-ONE

Servant of Darkness

"WHAT HAVE YOU DONE!" Ezamay rolled, making it off the counter to kneel next to her husband. Pulling his limp body against her, she hugged his head to her chest. Weeping loudly, she wailed, "Foolish child! You used a transference, didn't you!" She cut her eyes up at Sarah. "A curse upon you for this treachery."

"She's already cursed," Blake snapped, taking a knee beside her. "And this wasn't her choice. Garrett instructed we use the spell, despite our misgivings." With a steady hand, he pushed her fingers aside, feeling Garretts neck and cheek. "He lives," he announced with a breath of relief.

"No thanks to you," May bit angrily. "You shouldn't have done it. You should have found another way."

"There was no other way," Blake asserted. "Not with the resources we had at hand. Not with the time that remained." He caught her face, pressing gently at the base of her skull, his thumb tracing her ear. "We have done as your husband asked. Your curse is his to bear."

"What about my cancer? Does he carry that as well?" She sniffed, tears streaking her pink cheeks.

"I don't know, but I doubt it. You should heal though, with the vile mark removed," he speculated. "And with any luck, Garrett will not fall ill right away." Glancing up at Rider, he added, "Can you help lift him to the pallet? We can assess him there."

Reluctantly, Ezamay released her husband's body to them, and Rider took his feet. Blake hoisted his torso and they laid him upon the blankets. Sarah had moved the text and held the pillow, ready to place it beneath his head, had the older woman not snatched it away.

"I'll do that!" May snarled. "You've done enough already."

Timidly, Sara folded her hands in front of her, uncomfortable in the gown that had brought her peace only moments before. "I need to change," she announced, hurrying from the room before her tears were seen.

"Don't be so hard on her," Rider clipped. "We warned Garrett you wouldn't be happy."

Merideth sidled up to her mother, placing her left hand on her father's chest. "I told Daddy not to do it." Shedding her own drops of saddness, she curled Ezamay against her with the right, her arm holding her firmly.

"I'm the head of this family," Garret slurred. "I made the call."

"Garrett!" Ezamay squealed, the two women hugged each other joyfully.

His eyes opened a crack and he could make out their blurred forms. "Is it done?"

"It is," Blake assured him, giving his shoulder a squeeze. "You may need to rest, though."

"I believe I will," Garrett agreed. "This curse is… heavy. I feel the weight of it upon me."

"You can feel a curse?" Joseline asked innocently.

"Not normally." Blake shoved his hands in his pockets. "You're probably imagining it. Because you know it's there."

Garrett licked his lips, the mass on his chest giving him doubt. "How long will it take, do you think? For the cancer to grow?"

"I was sick for months." Ezamay swallowed, regaining her composure. "I will turn every stone in search of a cure. A real cure." She glared at those who surrounded her, unwilling to forgive them.

Leaving them, Karen slunk away, quietly climbing the stairs in search of her best friend. Locating her in the master suite, Sarah had removed the white gown, tossing it across the bed, and once again donned her customary jeans and tee. Her shoulder's shook, and with hands covering her face she drew ragged breaths.

"Sarah, honey," Karen quieted her. Reaching her, she ran a firm hand up the girl's back to console her.

"I shouldn't have done it." Sarah panted. "I told Blake it was wrong."

"But you had to," Karen argued, pulling her around to face her. "We couldn't let Meri's mom die!"

"Oh, but her dad can? Do you not see how messed up that is?" Sarah pulled away from her, remorse giving way to anger.

"There will be time to search for a way to save him," Karen assured. "We were frantic, with only hours left. We needed the delay moving the curse will bring."

"And what if we don't find the cure?" Sarah bowed

up to her, standing toe to toe. "Who gets it then? You?" She curled her fists, nails digging into her palms. "You have no idea what it's like, Karen. To carry a curse. To feel it inside, you. Growing. Changing you. With nothing you can do to stop it."

"Oh, Sarah," her friend breathed quietly. "I'm so sorry."

"Well, don't be. This was my fault. I was the caster. A servant of darkness. And again, I have destroyed another life." Flipping her bright red locks, she stomped out of the room.

TWENTY-TWO

Beggars and Choosers

"OH MY GOD, WHAT A DAY!" Blake groaned, stretching out across their bed. The clock to his right read twenty after eight, but it felt like midnight. In his typical bare feet and chest, he toyed with his hairs, tickling himself with the caress. He glanced at Sarah, who stood at the window, staring out into the darkness. "Are you ready to go to sleep?"

"No."

He sucked his lips into a perfect pucker. "You wanna fuck?" He pushed himself up onto an elbow, admiring the view. When she didn't respond, he swung his feet to the floor to go fishing in his bag. "I got us some new lube." He shook the box to rattle the tube inside.

She turned enough to glare at him. "Is this really where your mind is?"

"Always." He laughed, a salacious grin lingering. "It would take your mind off of things." He reached for her, pulling at her shirt. "I know you love it."

"I do love it," she snapped, stepping out of his grasp. "That's part of the problem."

His face fell. "I wasn't aware there was a problem with our sex life. If you have something to say, just come out with it." He toyed with the box, as if debating whether to open it.

"I want to have a baby with you," she snapped. "But the Brenna in me still wants you to fuck her in the ass. See the problem?"

"You want to have a baby?" His features softened.

"Oh, Blake." She threw up her hands in defeat. "I do. I really do, but—"

"There is no but," he cut her off. "I know today was shitty all the way around, but in the end, we did what we had to do. So, forget about Garrett and Ezamay. Leave the rest of the group out of this. This is you and me." He tossed the box on the dresser. Closing the distance between them, he pulled her against him, then pressed his lips to hers.

Her mouth opened, inviting him in. "I need you so bad," she moaned.

Snatching at her clothes, he stripped her. Not carefully, not gently. Raw desire drove him as he yanked her jeans down her legs. She panted, trying to help, his aggression fueling her fire. While she worked at getting her shirt and bra off, he was naked before her. Shoving her back against the bedding, he plunged inside her as the last article slipped from her hand.

His thrusts pure animal, he drove against her. "Blake," she grunted, her nails digging into his shoulders.

Using one hand to hold himself up, his other pushed at her legs, then slid up her body to her throat. His palm against her windpipe, he squeezed, preventing all but a gurgle from escaping her. "This is mine," he growled.

She bared her teeth, her breath pushing between them. When her face flushed, he released the pressure, laying his sweaty cheek next to hers as they panted in unison, their climax simultaneous.

BAM. BAM. BAM.

"What the fuck is that?" Blake rolled off of her, answering the door in all his naked glory.

"Have you even a shred of decency?" Rider demanded, his eyes fixed on the other man's face. "The rest of the house is trying to get some much-needed sleep."

"And we are having some much-needed sex." Blake closed the door with a slam. Stomping across the room, he seized the box, tearing at the end of it.

"We're not done?" Sarah asked, her breathing still not quite normal.

"Oh, no, Baby. Not by a long shot." Tossing the cardboard aside, he opened the tube, grinning at the gooey fluid. When he reached her, he flipped her over, dripping the lube and using his fingers to massage it in before inserting himself for round two.

Pushing back against him, her face twisted in a mixture of pleasure and pain. "Oh, dear God," she groaned. Clutching the blanket, her knuckles white, she sobbed, "Oh yes!" not caring who else in the house heard them.

Out in the hall, Rider heard Sarah's squaller as he reached their door. "Assholes," he muttered, slamming the portal once he had entered.

"You didn't have much luck," Merideth observed

with a small grin. Seated in the bed, the covers draped across her, she couldn't have appeared more elegant in her silk nighty.

"Nope. He's a real dick. He didn't even cover himself before he answered the door!"

"Did you expect him to?"

"What if it had been your mother!" Rider fumed, pulling off his pants and climbing in next to her.

"My mother has more sense than to knock on a door when she knows full well what they're doing on the other side," she quipped. "One might say you deserved it."

"Oh, I deserved it?" He turned over, catching her beneath him. "How are we supposed to get any sleep around here?"

"I guess we're not," she teased, pulling him down to her.

Their kiss lingering, he groaned. "It doesn't feel right doing the nasty in your parents' house."

"Then don't be nasty. Let's make love. Like we used to."

Their faces close, he nuzzled her, kissing her gently. "Can you do it quietly?"

She giggled. "Don't worry, Boo. No one will hear." Pushing him, she sat up, lifting her nightgown over her head to reveal her supple, naked curves beneath it.

"Well." He panted as her fingers splayed across his chest. "I guess we can make a little noise." Pulling her leg, he entered her smoothly, working her with his even thrust. She relaxed into him, their hands and mouths free to taste and explore in the dim light.

"Nope. Not done yet." Joseline giggled. In their bedroom across the hall from Sarah and Blake, she lay with an elbow propping her up, her free hand massaging the naked girl next to her.

"They can go for hours," Karen reminded her, heaving a sigh. "Sometimes I think all the noise is just for show."

Joseline trailed her jaw with gentle fingertips. "We make a fair amount of noise, ladybug."

"Maybe I couldn't hear it over all the racket." Karen laughed, catching Josee's digits and kissing them. "Have you ever been in love?" she asked quietly.

"Oh, Karen," Jos whispered. "It might be a little soon to be talking like that."

"I'm not saying that. I'm just curious. Don't get your panties in a wad," Karen teased.

"I'm not wearing any," the other girl quipped. Leaning closer, their lips gently suctioned together. Slithering down Karen's nakedness, she pushed against her thigh, working her way in. Her tongue agile, she tasted the sweetness of her puss, then lapped at her clit. Rubbing her folds, she mused, "We should get you pierced."

Karen winced. "Does it hurt?"

"Like a bitch." Jos pushed her tongue inside her, then flicked the tip over her swollen pea. "Afterwards, it feels great, though. You cum just walking sometimes."

"No way." Karen giggled, resting hand on Joseline's head. "If we're still together in a year, I'll get it pierced."

"Chicken." Josee pushed herself up, sitting to insert her fingers. "I'm going to make you cum just for that."

Relaxing her legs, Karen pulled at her knees to give her more room. "I get to do you next."

"Maybe." Jos leaned forward to kiss her. "We've got all night, ladybug."

Sitting in their swing in the back yard, a quilt surrounded Garrett and Ezamay as he held her. Naked, their skin stuck in places when they moved, but neither of them cared. It had been nearly a year since they made love, but this night it had been right.

"I hope we don't wake the kids when we go back in," May whispered, her head resting against his bare chest.

"I don't plan on going back in," he growled, kissing her forehead. "We'll just sleep under the stars, like we used to."

"Ah, but we were younger then." She smiled at the memory. "I'm still angry, you know."

"I know; but you'll forgive me. We've stolen a few more months together; and if that's all we get, it was worth it to me." He hugged her tighter. "I love you with all my heart, Ezamay."

"And I you." She sighed. "I do forgive you. And them, I guess."

"You should tell them that," he chided. "They need to know you are on their side."

"I'm not on anyone's side. This business with Morcant is absurd."

"He started it. He's always bullied Judoc, even when they were but wee little things," he recalled.

"I remember." She blinked a few times, her mind trapped in the past. "I will help him, Garrett. Don't worry. I won't let Morcant get away with any of this."

"I hope so, my sweet. I really hope so."

TWENTY-THREE

A Will and a Way

"WHAT'S THIS DOING HERE?" Sarah asked as she entered the kitchen, avoiding touching the long white gown hanging in the doorway. The last to come down, she noticed Alice didn't look very pleased from her position at the stove. They had cleaned up some of the mess, but the room wouldn't be its old self for weeks, more than likely.

"That is for you," Ezamay informed her, indicating the dress with an open palm. "I told you I wanted you to have it." Seated at the bar next to her husband, the rest of the group occupied chairs at the table behind them.

"I don't really think I should take it," Sarah replied, not looking at the other woman. Shuffling past the older couple, she took a chair next to Blake. Glancing around, the others appeared to be waiting for the meal as empty plates sat before them.

Joseline and Karen snuggled and smooched, while Rider and Meri sipped coffee and exchanged coy glances. "What is going on here?" Sarah whispered, leaning closer to her lover. Even the older couple at the bar seemed to be exchanging affection freely.

"It would appear that everyone had a good night," Blake observed, sliding his arm around her. "I hope you meant what you said."

"What did I say?" She looked at him blankly.

"About the baby," he elaborated. "I've put my seed inside you. There's no going back if it sticks."

"I'm ready." She flushed, glancing at the others. "I'm not sure of our timing, though. Morcant seems to be winning at this point."

"We will defeat him," Ezamay spoke up, standing to join them. "Where there's a will, there's a way." Turning to her second daughter, she added, "We'll need everyone, though."

"Does that mean you plan to join my coven?" Blake asked in surprise. Glancing over at Garrett, the older man had not moved, and sat drinking his brew as if he hadn't a care in the world.

"I'm not going to Boston, if that's what you're asking," Ezamay said stiffly. "But I wouldn't mind being consulted from time to time." She nodded, glancing at the others. "Your brother fucked up when he came at me." Her words sharp, the group adjusted in their seats. Noticing their discomfort, she chuckled. "I'm a tough old woman. Morcant will certainly get his if I can help it."

"What about you guys?" Blake raised his chin at the couple across from him.

"We don't have much of a choice, now do we," Rider shot back. "But I'm not putting up with this 'magister' bullshit. You're not my boss." He pointed at the other man for good measure.

"That's not how covens work," Sarah said quietly.

"Exactly," Karen chimed, rolling her eyes before returning to caressing Joseline's arm.

Blake glared at him. "If you join us, I'll expect you to take direction." He tapped the table with a knuckle. "However, I am in the market for an enforcer. Someone to help guard the coven against attacks."

"Sounds like a shit job." Rider smirked. "Meri and I are going home. We'll let you know."

"Fair enough." Blake gave a slight nod. "Don't think too long, though. Garrett's condition won't keep, and we'll need to find the counter for it before he becomes as ill as May was."

"And there's the matter of Joseline's amulet," Karen pointed out, sitting up straighter. "We still need a way of removing it from her."

"And we can't forget about Brenna." Sarah sighed. "She's locked away at the moment, but with Morcant pushing buttons, it's only a matter of time before he finds the right one."

Alice arrived at the table, a platter of sausage, bacon, biscuits and gravy in her hands. "Shall I serve?"

"No, put the dish on the table and we'll help ourselves," Ezamay suggested.

Leaving his seat at the bar, Garrett joined them, each taking a portion of the meal while Alice topped off their coffee cups, then left them to their meal.

Once they had started to eat, Garrett cleared his throat. "I've been considering my decision to remain a bystander."

The group paused, lowing their forks and staring at

the older man. "Have you changed your mind, Daddy?" Meri's eyes wide, she held her breath.

"I don't know what I can do to help." He shrugged. "I know enough to know I wouldn't be much good with positions and casting. But I can offer a haven. You are all welcome here, and you may use this house as you see fit. And of course, all of the family tomes are yours, Merideth." He held out a flat hand towards her, as if handing them over.

"Thank you, Daddy," she said more confidently. She cut her eyes over at her mate, waiting for him to speak up. When he did not, she grunted, elbowing him.

Chewing his food, Rider didn't budge. He wasn't ready to commit, so she wasn't going to goad him into it.

Seeing the display, Ezamay grinned at him. "You are a stubborn man, Rider Bradshaw. I believe you get that from your father."

"I don't get anything from my old man," Rider stated curtly. "Speaking of which, why don't you ask him to come be your enforcer. I bet he'd jump at that. A chance to be in the thick of things."

"He may already be in the thick of things," Blake growled.

"What do you mean?" Meri asked, dropping her fork.

"My brother is getting help from the outside. It could be him," Blake stated flatly, his eyes fixed on Rider.

"It could be anyone," Joseline pointed out, sensing their tempers rising.

"If you think my father is working against you, why would you want us in your coven?" Rider glared back at him.

"Merideth, I'm afraid your boyfriend isn't being very cooperative," Blake stated calmly.

"He seldom is," she observed, glancing between them. "I want to join them, Boo. You go back to NOLA if that's what you want to do, but my sister and mother need me." She cut her brown orbs over at Garrett. "And my father needs me. I'm a witch, after all. I can't pretend it away."

Blake grinned at her choice, surprised she had made it. "Welcome, Meri." He squinted at his rival. "Up to you," he clipped, pushing for a decision.

Rider's gaze swung to her and he studied her for a long moment. The others resumed their eating but the two of them sat in silence, each waiting for the other to change their mind. Rider was the first to crack. "Is this really what you want? We won't have a life of our own if we do this." He had seen the world of magic from the inside and considered himself lucky to have escaped it.

"Like you said, what choice do we have?" She fidgeted with the napkin in her lap. "Either we join or we say goodbye to the people we care about as Morcant picks them off one by one."

Rider nodded, understanding what she meant, as well as how much she really had to lose.

"All right," he groaned, leaning back in his chair. "I'll be your damned enforcer." Pushing the seat back, he stood. "I'll book us on a flight to New Orleans so we can pack up there, and then we'll meet you in Boston in a few weeks." He left the room, his shoulder's hunched as if he'd been beaten.

"If you think Thaddeus is part of Morcant's followers, are you sure we can trust him?" Karen asked doubtfully.

"We need every hand we can get," Blake observed. "Besides, Rider seems dead set against everything his father stands for. If that old man's taken Morcant's side, that just means his son will fight even harder against him."

Merideth placed her elbows on the table and leaned against her hands. "I hope you're right. As the seer of our little group, I feel I should warn you, I fear our fight has only just begun."

Epilogue

"WHAT THE FUCK?" Morcant grunted to himself when he entered the visitation chamber. Across the room, the man seated at the table could not have surprised him more. Working his way between the tables and chairs, he took a seat facing his brother. "Judoc. What are you doing here?"

"Not who you expected, huh?" Blake grinned at him, ignoring his use of his old moniker.

"What makes you think I was expecting anyone," Morcant tossed back.

"Because I know what you've done," Blake replied sharply. "The curse has been removed from Ezamay. Her cancer is in remission."

"That's good to hear. Cancer sucks." Morcant shrugged. "What makes you think she was cursed?"

"Stop playing dumb." Blake leaned towards him. "I know you've been casting."

"I'm in prison. You think I can reach you and your silly friends from here?"

"I want you to stop messing with our lives." Blake stabbed the table with a stiff digit. "This is the only warning you're going to get."

"Or what? You'll break into prison and beat me up?" Morcant mocked.

"Curses go both ways," Blake challenged, aware that might be true but he had far more to lose.

A slow smile spread across the older sibling's lips. "When's she due?"

The color drained from Blake's face. "I have no idea what you're talking about."

"Sure, you do. The seed of our line has been planted. Did you think I wouldn't know? I'm the magister of our coven, regardless of what you call yourself." With a twisted grin, Morcant waited for the reply.

Blake studied him. He and Sarah had begun trying to conceive their last night in Virginia. As it was scarcely three weeks ago, he had no evidence they had succeeded. Holding a straight face, he denied, "Believe what you will, but heed my warning. I will come for you, brother." Standing, he waved to the guard, signaling their conversation was finished.

"This isn't over, Judoc," Morcant snarled, also getting to his feet. "You should watch your back. You never know who might want to stick a knife in it," he called to him as the guard led him away.

Thank You

Thank you for sharing in this magical adventure! Please be sure to leave a review and don't miss the next installment of the Unexpected Magic Series ~ Sam

Books in this series include:
    The Binding (book 1)
    The Wicked Awakened (book 2)
    The Secret Sibling (book 3)
    The Whisperer (book 4)
    The Magister's Child (book 5)

Boxed Sets
    The Unexpected Magical Opening Duo (books 1 and 2)

About the Author

Anyone who knows me could tell you, I am a friendly kind of person, never met a stranger and take up conversations anywhere at any time. I work hard, and my mind never seems to shut down, as I wake up often in the middle of the night with ideas pouring out and demanding to be dealt with. Of course that means much of my books were written in the middle of the night.

I grew up and still live in the great state of Texas where everything is bigger, where we have warm weather and a central location. I love my state, my town, and my family, which includes my four sons, my significant other, and many friends as well.

I have thoroughly enjoyed writing this story and hope that you will love reading it just as much. And of course, there will be many more adventures to come.

You can follow Samantha Jacobey at:
Website: www.SamJacobey.com
Facebook: https://www.facebook.com/SamJacobey
Twitter: https://twitter.com/SamJacobey

Also by SAMANTHA JACOBEY

A New Life Series

http://myBook.to/ANewLifeSeries

An epic adventure, TORI FARRELL's life IS one wild story... escaped from a biker gang and running from drug lords... used by the FBI and hoping to protect her present from her past... IT'S DARK - IT'S BRUTAL, and it's WORTH EVERY MINUTE OF IT!! (Mature Adult, 18+)

Summer Spirit Novella Series

http://myBook.to/SummerSpiritSeries

No one EVER had a summer romance like this… Charlie visits another plane, parallel to our own, where Summer Angels and Dark Angels battle over the fate of man. A unique twist on an old idea that will keep you guessing; will Charlie and Clarisse ever find their HEA? (New adult)

Irrevocable Series

http://mybook.to/IrrevocableBoxedSet

From affluent beginnings, BAILEY DEWITT's life has become a broken mess... after her parents died unexpectedly, she didn't think it could get any worse. But when the arrogance of man catches up and puts the entire world into a dooms-day spiral, there will be only ONE PLACE she can run to - the ONE PLACE she wanted desperately to escape. (New Adult)

Teach Me to Prey

http://hyperurl.co/e9qs9f

In this standalone thriller, JASON TRUITT and his friends have gotten their way for years. Deceit, sex, and foul play aren't normally covered in the curriculum, but they're doing whatever it takes to get under BECKY STEWART's skin. When one of the boys turns up dead, it's a race against time to save the others; a STUNNING STORY that will get your heart racing and leave you breathless by the end… (New Adult)

The Wicked Awakened

http://hyperurl.co/2qsgl6

A Halloween novel; a five-hundred-year-old witch wants to turn SARAH MATTHEWS' body into her new home… A twisted tale involving a coven hell bent on seeing that she succeeds. Who will come out on top in this epic battle of wills? (Mature Adult, 18+)

The Binding

http://myBook.to/TheBinding

One cursed diary will change two strangers forever…Can Meri and Rider use her mother's old book to figure out why someone is after them? Or will the guilty party succeed, ripping the tome away before killing them and then slithering back into the darkness…

Also from the Lavish family

The Norn Novellas
A. Nicky Hjort
http://myBook.to/NornNovellas

The Norn Novellas are all chapters in the epic saga of the youngest and most fickle of the four Norn Sisters. The same feisty immortal creature who must escape her inherent inner darkness to learn the meaning of life.

Each story takes a classic fairytale and spins it on its head, as we learn that maybe Norse Mythology was so much more than legend. And to think, you thought you knew those old tales so well.

Meet Za and find out what really happened...

When Tundra Turns to Ardnyt - Book 1: In the center of a magical world there grows a beautiful and terrible chasm of climbing plants. On one side of the Ivy Wall we find the hell-of-Tyndra, on the other, the heaven-of-Ardnyt. But legend has it that in the middle…lives a preternatural beast that imprisons and tortures the children from both sides.

When the war against time begins, Azza will have to cross over the Ivy Wall, something that has never been done before by a living being. But if she does make it through, she just might discover who she really is and how she became trapped in this alternate reality.

A fairytale at heart, this is the first chapter in the epic saga of the youngest and most fickle of the four Norn Sisters. The same feisty immortal creature who must escape her inherent inner darkness to learn the meaning of love.

A veritable palindrome from start to finish, the narrative of Where Tyndra Turns to Ardnyt journeys through duality to discover what shocking truths emerge when up becomes down, life becomes death, suffering becomes release, and the most unexpected endings become the most surprising beginnings.

Welcome to a place where forwards and backwards are exactly the same direction. Here Where Tyndra Turns to Ardnyt.

Where Ebon Sounds Like Ivory – book 2: Norse legend has it that the arms of the Yggdrasil tree—a sacred instrument of Odin—are ever-reaching, and its survival is necessary for life itself to continue.

During Winter's Solstice, when the search for her mortal mother begins, Za will have to cross over the Ebon Branch of the Dead—a feat that has supposedly never been survived intact. But if she does make it across and back home, she just might discover why she and the other three Norn Sisters of Fate came to be.

A fairytale at heart, this is the second chapter in the epic saga of the youngest and most fickle of the four Norn Sisters. The same feisty immortal creature who must discover her true origins to understand her inherent inner darkness. Only this way can she learn the meaning of unconditional sacrifice in the name of impenetrable love…when, as her destiny would have it, all the branches of such a powerful tree tremble treacherously in her tiny little hands.

A veritable unraveling of Snow White, the narrative of Where Ebon Sounds Like Ivory journeys through the most horrible of realms where shocking truths emerge. Here where death mimics life, obsession masquerades as devotion, and the most unexpected endings become the most surprising beginnings of a classic tale. One…you thought you knew so well.

Welcome to a place where the darkest of melodies births a miraculous tune of surrenderance. Here Where Ebon Sounds Like Ivory and Christmas, as we know it, begins.

Behind Blue Eyes Series
Sara J. Bernhardt
http://mybook.to/BehindBlueEyesSeries

A father's desire to save his child presents him with an unthinkable choice that leaves him darker than human, forced to roam through time alone as he searches for the place he belongs.

Adam Gold – Book 1: Fleeing the French invasion of Geneva Switzerland in the 1700s, Adam Gold books passage to America with his family. On the ship, Adam's daughter falls fatally ill. A mysterious man comes to Adam with a way to save his child by turning Adam into something darker than human.

The Medallion – Book 2: Adam Gold, an immortal with sweet eyes of blue, rushes through the centuries on a quest for reason and a thirst for revenge. To cope with his pain and regret, he sleeps away the years and awakes in a new era with a powerful, ancient vampire who sets her sights on him.

Golden Shackles – Book 3: When the ancient queen, Sekhmet snatches up Adam, he is faced with a terrifying decision. To help aid her in her vile plans or dare to stand against her.

Plus 3 more segments!